THE CASE
OF THE
ILL-FATED
Playwright

FRED W. EDMISTON

ISBN: 1450540708
ISBN-13: 9781450540704

PREFACE

I long deferred including this narrative among my chronicles of the remarkable talents of Mr. Sherlock Holmes. In the first place, it is unique among my good friend's professional cases and was one in which he had a somewhat secondary role. Moreover, the details of Mr. Oscar Wilde's tragic downfall have, until recently, remained so controversial that it has not been practical to describe them for a public still reluctant to deal with matters of this character. However, more than three decades have passed since that terrible winter and spring of 1895. Mr. Wilde has been dead nearly thirty years, and Holmes has recently died. Also, I know that I cannot reasonably expect more than a modest amount of time remaining to me. There was thus only a limited opportunity to set down, in an organised account, my own and Sherlock Holmes's roles in those events that so occupied much of the world's attention at the end of the last century. Both the Wilde *cause célèbre* and Holmes's association with it are unquestionably interesting. Despite my belief, however, that the story should be told, I now find myself in a physical condition that makes problematic my doing the work that a creditable narrative requires.

It is fortunate that as I struggled with this matter, I happened to mention my quandary to an acquaintance who knew someone very willing to work with me on such an undertaking. My friend described this man as not only a capable writer but also one of Wilde's closest friends and, therefore, thoroughly familiar with the subject. Thus it was that I became associated with Mr. Reginald Turner, whom I recalled seeing once or twice during the months preceding the government's prosecution of Mr. Wilde, and for a brief period afterward. This kind, amiable, and witty man helped to organise my data and to add much of his own recollecting. He provided information about events to which I was not privy and also made possible a fuller, more accurate and distinctive treatment of the remarkable story.

This account is, therefore, a product of several hands; for in addition to what Mr. Turner brings to it, much helpful information has come from such others as Mrs. Ada Esther Leverson, Mme. Fariedeh Marisepehr, and from Messrs. Robert Baldwin Ross, Frank Harris, Bernard Shaw, and William More Adey. Mr. Ross died in 1918 and Mr. Turner now lives abroad.

For compositional reasons, in this narrative I refer to myself in the third person.

John H. Watson, M. D.

Chapter 1

M r. Sherlock Holmes and Dr. John H. Watson, especially
the latter, had read and heard about Oscar Wilde and his
brilliant literary and dramatic successes. They knew also of
his distinguished work as both editor and critic. Several of his
essays had attracted their attention; and his novel, *The Picture
of Dorian Gray*, took the nation quite by surprise and received
both strong praise and bitter condemnation. The book was
deucedly witty and imaginative but, as some thought, also un-
wholesome. It seemed to illustrate Wilde's aphorism: "When
critics disagree the artist is in accord with himself." The novel
was quickly followed by two very successful comedies, *A Woman
of No Importance* and *Lady Windermere's Fan*. Holmes and
Watson attended these productions and laughed throughout
each play's sparkling acts. Both works represented nothing less
than a revival of a genre not seen in England since the great
comedies by such Restoration and eighteenth century drama-
tists as William Congreve and Richard Sheridan. In late 1894

the British public read with delight of the imminent presentation, at the Haymarket Theatre, of the author's third comedy. And at almost the same time there was further excited anticipation at the announcement that Wilde had nearly finished a fourth play. This was *The Importance of Being Earnest*, which many now regard as the author's masterpiece. Thus, by February of 1895 Mr. Wilde had two highly successful comedies running simultaneously at two of London's best theatres. But on the heels of these successes occurred their author's abrupt descent from his pinnacle. It was a fall unprecedented in British literary and social history, one that clearly surpassed Lord Byron's.

On New Year's Day, 1895, shortly after Holmes and Watson had finished breakfast, they relaxed in their parlour. Watson occupied the sofa and perilously balanced a cup of coffee with one hand while scanning several issues of *The Times* with the other. Holmes sat some distance away at his worktable where, puffing on his pipe, he did research for a monograph on criminal physiognomy.

A knock on the door made Holmes look up and exclaim, "Come in!" Their landlady, Mrs. Hudson, appeared and said that a young gentleman wished to see Holmes. She handed Watson the visitor's card, which he examined and then read aloud.

"*Mr. Robert Baldwin Ross.* Are you expecting anyone of that name, Holmes?"

"No, the name is unfamiliar. Thank you, Mrs. Hudson. Please show him in."

Watson set his cup down and hurried to pick up several pages of the newspaper that he had casually strewn about. The young man who entered was tastefully dressed and rather young, certainly not older than his mid-twenties. Though pleasant of visage and manner, his general appearance was unremarkable; and his medium-brown hair was beginning to recede above his forehead.

"Good morning, Mr. Ross. I'm Dr. John Watson and that is my associate, Mr. Sherlock Holmes."

The visitor bowed slightly to each man. "Dr. Watson, Mr. Holmes, how do you do? Thank you for receiving me, and I hope my arriving without an appointment is not inconvenient." Ross was agreeably reserved and used gestures modestly. His speech and poise suggested a genteel background.

Watson shook the visitor's hand. Holmes, who had risen from his worktable on the far side of the room, nodded slightly and gave the hint of a smile.

"Won't you sit down, Mr. Ross?" exclaimed Holmes as he gestured toward a chair. Ross seated himself, and Watson returned to his place on the sofa. Holmes moved to his favorite chair and, settling leisurely into it, continued to smoke his pipe.

There followed several minutes of general conversation during which Holmes made a keen study of their visitor. Watson was aware of Holmes's scrutiny and tried to emulate it. After about ten minutes Holmes abruptly said: "And now, Mr. Ross, I assume this is not a social call. How may we help you? I assure you that you may speak confidentially before both Dr. Watson and myself."

Nodding, and with a smile to Watson, Ross reached inside his coat and brought out an envelope. "Gentlemen, this is a letter from my friend, Mr. Oscar Wilde, who would be honoured if both of you would accept his invitation to dine tomorrow at Kettner's. He hopes also that you will accept two reservations in the dress circle at the Theatre Royal, Haymarket, on Thursday, January third—the day after tomorrow. It will be the first night of Mr. Wilde's new play, *An Ideal Husband.*"

Holmes rose, took the envelope from Ross, and resumed his seat. After scanning the invitation, he said: "Mr. Ross, I shall send Mr. Wilde a written reply. Meanwhile, please inform him that as grateful as I am for his kind offer, my schedule at present is somewhat tight. And while I have every intention of seeing this new play at some convenient time, I must ask that he excuse me at present. Now, Watson, there is no reason why you should not avail yourself of Mr. Wilde's kindness on both occasions."

Watson was in a quandary as to how to respond to Holmes. He was even more discomfited by the obvious disappointment visible on the young visitor's face. "Well, Holmes, I certainly have no intention of deserting you. Besides, I have a patient who may very well need my services throughout the rest of this week."

"Well, suit yourself, my dear fellow, but I think you might well take some time off."

Watson turned to the visitor. "Mr. Ross, please tell your friend that while we have no intention of missing even one of his excellent plays, a date sometime in the middle of January might be more practical for both Mr. Holmes and me."

Ross was clearly frustrated. "Gentlemen, I'm sure that can be arranged, though I think Mr. Wilde expects to leave London in about a fortnight for a trip to Algiers. He was hoping very particularly to see both of you at your earliest convenience."

"When does Mr. Wilde expect to return?" asked Holmes.

"I'm not certain, but I think he plans to be gone two or three weeks."

Holmes nodded. "I'm sure that would be satisfactory with both of us. In the meantime, Mr. Ross, you will, I trust, be sure to tell Mr. Wilde that I shall write him a suitable reply explaining fully our present inability to accept his generous invitations."

Ross chuckled softly. "Gentlemen, it is true that Mr. Wilde is generous, but I assure you that there's more than generosity in his invitation. If I may so put it, I'd say that there is quite a lot of self-interest in it. Indeed, he had hoped to ask you, Mr. Holmes, to help him solve a mystery that just at present complicates his life."

Holmes stopped puffing on his pipe and slowly leaned forward. "Indeed, Mr. Ross? What sort of mystery?"

"Well, I can't give you the details. For one thing, I myself don't know them all. Furthermore, I'm sure that Mr. Wilde can explain much more effectively." Ross smiled and added, "He is, after all, a master of language."

In the moment of silence that followed, Holmes's curiosity was obvious. Suddenly he laid his pipe down and turned to his associate. "Watson, what is the status of that matter involving Sir Charles Richbrook?"

"We're waiting for a reply from Sir Charles. Until we hear from him, we can do nothing."

Sinking back into his chair, Holmes clasped his hands behind his head and looked thoughtful. "I've made good progress on my work today and have no other pressing matters on the outside." He paused, then looked at Watson with a somewhat exaggerated show of concern: "My dear fellow, you of course are the medical authority; but I think you really have been pushing yourself mercilessly. You should take the same excellent care of yourself that you do of your patients." The detective looked over at their visitor. "Mr. Ross, on second thought I believe we both should avail ourselves of your friend's kind invitation."

"I'm delighted, Mr. Holmes! I hope that will be for both the dinner and the theatre?"

"Oh, yes indeed! Good entertainment is always enhanced by a good dinner."

"But," said Ross with a smile, "remember that they're a day apart."

"So much the better. Then each can be more intelligently savoured."

Ross laughed and said, "Yes, I've heard Oscar—I beg your pardon—I've heard Mr. Wilde say that after a good dinner one can forgive anyone, even one's own relatives!"

"Ha! Watson, I must remember that! Perhaps I shall test the theory on Lestrade sometime."

"Lestrade?" asked the visitor.

"Oh, just one of Scotland Yard's functionaries," said Holmes with a dismissive gesture. Watson had difficulty suppressing a laugh.

Ross nodded uncertainly and replied: "Well, Mr. Holmes and Dr. Watson, I must not intrude further on your time. I am most grateful for your willingness to see me. I speak both for myself and Mr. Wilde in saying that we shall be delighted to see you tomorrow evening at Kettner's and the next evening at the Haymarket."

The three men rose; and as Ross turned to leave, Holmes said, "Mr. Ross, one moment, please. Has Mr. Wilde sought police assistance?"

"No, not yet."

"I see." Holmes beamed and exclaimed, "Couldn't have done better!"

Robert Ross bowed slightly to both men and left. Holmes strode over to a window from which he observed Ross engage and enter a hansom. He saw also a somewhat heavily cloaked man who watched closely as their recent visitor got into his cab. After Ross's hansom left, the mysterious observer entered a second cab and left in the same direction.

"Well, Watson," said Holmes as he returned to his chair, "it appears that Mr. Ross has touched a tender nerve with someone."

"What do you mean?"

"That he apparently was followed here and is being followed leaving here." Holmes reoccupied his chair and after musing for a moment asked, "What did you think of our visitor?"

Watson shrugged. "He seems personable, articulate, and well mannered—and almost ostentatiously young." Struggling to add to his observations, he said, "The young man is apparently convinced that Mr. Wilde is in some danger." After a pause he looked keenly at his friend. "And what did you conclude?"

"Not much beyond what you did, which suggests that young Mr. Ross has already learned to dissemble. That, in turn, suggests that there are aspects of his personality which he believes *must* be concealed."

"And do you find any clues as to what they might be?"

Holmes relit his pipe and took a long draught from it. "Nothing definite as yet. Besides, we must not let our imaginations mislead us. I notice that Mr. Ross has traces of a Canadian accent, and two or three things he said suggest that he has attended Cambridge. Beyond that I could only theorise."

Watson added, "I would say that he cares very deeply for Mr. Wilde."

Holmes nodded and, between puffs, murmured, "Which is suggestive."

Around noon, in a restaurant near Piccadilly Circus, a middle-aged, short, stocky man sat alone at a table. He clearly was expecting company, for he keenly observed everyone who entered and even those who merely passed outside. John

Sholto Douglas, Marquess of Queensberry, was not apprehensive of being disturbed by unexpected company; for everyone in London who knew him regarded him as, at the very least, eccentric—at worst, insane. He had few inhibitions. Indeed, he thought no more of engaging in fisticuffs with one of his sons on a London street than he did of denouncing, on the floor of the House of Lords, that august body's old traditions as "Christian tomfoolery."

No, Queensberry's disquiet arose from his concern that his coconspirator might be late or might have failed to get the information necessary in a schedule of retribution. The issue had become an obsession for Queensberry, and time was important. He did not have to wait long before Sean McConnell, a London policeman in civilian attire, entered the restaurant, saw the marquess, and quickly joined him. Queensberry waved him to a seat.

McConnell was about six feet tall. He had a ruddy complexion and thick, black hair which was cut short. His athletic physique, enhanced by active police work, matched his vigorous gestures. Queensberry found him congenial and increasingly useful in his effort to track the movements of Wilde and Lord Alfred Douglas.

As soon as the policeman had taken his seat, Queensberry said: "Well, McConnell, I hope you have something for me. But before you tell me, let me say that Wilde has apparently contacted that so-called *consulting* detective, Sherlock Holmes."

"How did you find that out, my lord?"

"I followed his stooge, Robert Ross, there this morning. He stayed about fifteen minutes." Queensberry tapped the table with his index finger. "If Holmes gets involved, it's going to make our work much harder."

"Why can't we do something to discourage the detective's interference?"

Queensberry shook his head. "It's not that easy; I know something of Sherlock Holmes. Once he starts anything, he won't give up until he's finished it. He's like a mastiff!" Queensberry laughed bitterly and added, "But I don't think that even the famous Mr. Sherlock Holmes will be able to protect Wilde from the facts that I'm going to have." He looked keenly at McConnell: "So, what kind of luck have you had with those young men? Will they be willing to give evidence if it comes to a trial?"

"Well, one or two seem interested if we pay them—they do indeed. But the others are very reluctant to get involved in any legal proceedings."

"And you did offer all of them money?"

"Yes, my lord, but I think it's going to take more than I felt free to offer. We may have to threaten them with prosecution if they don't cooperate."

"And by God we'll do it!" exclaimed Queensberry. "We need to get their kind off the streets, anyway." More calmly he asked, "What else have you found out?"

"My lord, I definitely believe I'll shortly have several pieces of correspondence that Wilde has written to—I beg your lordship's pardon—to Lord Alfred Douglas."

Queensberry reared back in his chair and said as loudly as even he dared in a public restaurant: "Don't bother to spare my feelings about that so-called son of mine!" A couple at a nearby table, startled by the speaker's vehemence, glanced over at him. Queensberry glared at them, and they quickly rediscovered an interest in what was on their plates. "Who has these letters?"

"Three of the young men."

"I want those letters!" said Queensberry loudly enough to earn a briefer and more cautious glance from the same neighbouring table. "So, do whatever you have to do to get them."

"I believe they have some sort of plan to extort money from Wilde. They believe Wilde will be willing to pay to get them back."

Queensberry hissed: "I don't want Wilde or anybody else but me to get them! That's the very sort of evidence I need!"

"I'll do my best, my lord, but I understand that one of them has already sent a copy of one letter to Herbert Tree, manager of the Haymarket Theatre."

"Well, do everything you can to get them. And, McConnell, *get the originals!*"

"Yes, my lord."

"Good! Now we need to get to work."

The two men started out, and as they reached the pavement, two well-known actors, Charles Hawtrey and Charles Brookfield, walked past. They noticed Queensberry and slowed down somewhat. Queensberry saw them glance back, and he signaled to them and told McConnell to go on without him. The marquess then walked over to the two men.

"Good to see both of you. I was delighted to receive your letter, Brookfield."

"Well, my lord, Mr. Hawtrey and I are both completely in sympathy with your efforts to bring Wilde down from his highhorse. And we think we can help even more than we already have."

"Wonderful! Wonderful!" exclaimed Queensberry. "I can certainly use all the help I can get." He drew both men over to the inside edge of the pavement and spoke quietly and confidentially. "Now, if all my plans work right, I'll be able to stop Oscar's career before the winter's quite over." He laughed quietly. "Wouldn't *that* be satisfying!"

"It would indeed, Lord Queensberry," said Hawtrey, "and we are ready to do everything in our power to help you."

Queensberry smiled. "You aren't afraid that you'd lose work if we send Oscar to gaol?"

"Hardly, my lord. I'm playing that role in Wilde's new play because I don't really have much choice. But I'd like it to be my last role in anything he writes."

"So would I," exclaimed Brookfield. "That's why I took the role of a butler in his new play. It required memorising very few of his lines." This made all three men chuckle.

"Well, Brookfield, Hawtrey, let's run over to my hotel where we can talk privately. You can then explain what you think you can do, and perhaps I can make some suggestions. And I'll let you know something of what *I'm* doing.

"Very good," said Brookfield. "Then Your Lordship would perhaps do us the honour of having lunch with us."

"I thank you," said Queensberry, "but I have a rather important errand to run. In fact, if it works out, I'll tell the two of you about it." He gestured with his head and said, "However, let's run by my hotel for a few minutes, and I'll give you some recent information." With that the three men moved off together.

After the two actors had left his suite, Queensberry took a cab to an address near Cavendish Square. The driver stopped in front of an attractive residence, and Queensberry got out, looked quickly about the neighborhood, and then rechecked the address he had written on a piece of paper. He paid the cabbie and stepped up to the door that bore a small metal sign: "Palmist and Advisor." Satisfied that he was at the correct address, he seized the knocker and banged it, then immediately repeated the action. He heard the door being opened. A very comely woman of Middle Eastern appearance confronted Queensberry and took him quite by surprise. It also quickened his resolve to let nothing distract him from the purpose of his visit.

"How do you do? Are you"—Queensberry checked his paper again—"Madame Marisepehr?"

"I am Madame Ma-RI-se-pehr."

"Ah! Indeed. I beg your pardon." Queensberry carefully pronounced her name as she had said it. He was struck by the woman's dark beauty that was enhanced by her heavily accented, but otherwise excellent, English.

"It is my understanding, Madame, that you cast horoscopes and perform palmistry."

"That is correct. Is that the reason for your visit?"

Queensberry nodded. "It's what I'd like to ask you about."

"Won't you come inside?"

The marquess entered with some hesitation, though this was quickly dissipated by the splendid appearance of the large foyer and adjoining reception room. He noticed also another dark-complexioned woman sitting in the room, but she quickly rose and excused herself. Madame Marisepehr bade her visitor to be seated, and she took a chair facing him.

"May I know *your* name, sir?"

"I am Lord Queensberry."

"And how may I help your lordship?"

Queensberry paused briefly to find the best way to proceed. "I believe that one of your clients is Oscar Wilde. Is this correct?"

Marisepehr was momentarily silent but then said, "My lord, I am reluctant to discuss my clients with third parties."

"Of course," said the marquess, "and that is very commendable. But I mean no harm to either you or those who consult you." He reached inside his coat, brought out his wallet, and extracted some currency. Marisepehr's eyes widened at the sight, and Queensberry played enticingly with several of the notes. "How much do you charge, Madame, for a consultation?"

"Sir, I would charge you five guineas for up to a half-hour."

"Ah, guineas!"

"Yes, my lord, I'm a professional."

"Of course, Madame, and your fee certainly is satisfactory." Queensberry first looked at his watch and then counted out the money, which he handed to Marisepehr.

She took it and looked at a clock nearby. "And now, Lord Queensberry, would you like me to cast your fortune?"

"No, Madame, I'm more interested in Mr. Wilde's fortune."

"I don't understand."

"I shall explain. May I assume that you will grant me that same confidence that you have said you give all your clients?"

"Of course, my lord."

Queensberry then quickly explained to her his desire to induce Wilde to take him to court.

"But why would Mr. Wilde wish to take you to court? And why do *you* wish him to do so?"

"Because, my dear lady, he has been interfering with my relations with my son. I intend to give him cause to charge me with libel or slander, and I'm convinced that I have enough evidence to defeat any charges he could make."

"Lord Queensberry, what is your son's age?"

"Lord Alfred is twenty-four."

"Fully adult, I believe. My lord, is not your son responsible for his own actions?"

Queensberry shook his head. "Most men of that age would be, but I fear that my son is not. He is immature and easily influenced, and Mr. Wilde is not a *wholesome* influence."

Marisepehr stared at the marquess for a moment. Then she rose and for several seconds strode about the room. Turning back to her visitor, she said, "My lord, I still don't quite understand what you wish me to do."

Queensberry leaned forward and in a confidential tone said, "Mr. Wilde will very likely ask your advice in this matter. And even if he does not, I'd like you to steer him to the subject and to assure him that he will win his case against me."

Marisepehr was clearly uncomfortable. Shaking her head vigourously, she exclaimed, "Sir, it would be unprofessional and against my principles to mislead a client."

"Well, Madame Marisepehr, I certainly understand and admire your integrity and your wish to deal honourably with those who trust your advice. But I'm only trying to protect my son's welfare. If I'm successful, that will be the result, and then both Mr. Wilde and I will go our separate ways—no great harm to anyone."

The palmist still balked and shook her head. Queensberry again withdrew his wallet and began thumbing through the money in it. "I would certainly not expect you to do this without compensation." He took out several of the notes and proceeded to count them slowly. "How does twenty-five pounds strike you?" She still wavered. "I'm so sorry! Did I say twenty-five? I meant fifty."

He counted out twenty-five more pounds, and her eyes twinkled. A perceptible smile appeared on her face. "My lord, I don't know quite what to say."

"Well—shall we *say* seventy-five pounds?" He laughed and added, "Oh, let's not quibble. I'll pay you a hundred pounds." He stopped, thought about it, and added, "And I'll pay you another hundred pounds if you *succeed* in persuading Mr. Wilde to charge me with libel or slander."

Marisepehr assured Queensberry that she thought she could do what he requested. "But, my lord, may I have that in guineas? I am, after all, a professional."

Queensberry gazed admiringly at the woman and, rising to leave, asked suggestively, "In what capacity, Madame?"

"Your lordship's wish is my command."

He smiled. "Is it, indeed? Well, perhaps when I bring you the second hundred pounds—I mean *guineas*. Then you may tell *my* fortune."

She smiled amiably.

That evening, at the home of Ernest and Ada Leverson, several guests enjoyed that gracious couple's hospitality. Chief among the visitors was Oscar Wilde, who often had been befriended by the Leversons. In addition to Robert Ross there was another young man, Reginald Turner, a journalist and wit, and the natural son of Edward Lawson, editor of the *Daily Telegraph*. The two other visitors were writer and artist Charles Rickets, and artistic designer Charles Shannon. The Leversons were among Wilde's favorite acquaintances. Especially as his personal problems increased and became ominous, he found the Leversons accommodating and comforting. Wilde affectionately referred to Ada Leverson as the Sphinx; and though Wilde often described women as sphinxes without secrets, he believed that Leverson's main secret was where in this imperfect world she had found her charm. She was gracious, witty, and intelligent.

The group chatted informally as they enjoyed drinks. Mrs. Leverson lightly commented that Wilde recently seemed preoccupied. "I hope your health remains good, Oscar."

"Sphinx, my physician gives me encouraging reports, prescribes absurd medicines, and charges fantastic fees. I assume that, like the ancient Roman physicians, he boasts that his patients never get well and do not die. But Madame Fariedeh Marisepehr, my spiritualist advisor, assures me that I have an unclouded future."

Ross laughed and exclaimed, "Oscar, of course she's going to tell you things like that! Why do you take her seriously?"

"Robbie, Robbie! You must remember that I'm an orthodox agnostic, so superstition is an important part of my canon. Besides, my poor, charming Sibyl must make a living; and she certainly can't expect to be paid for forecasting disaster." He chuckled. "She pays me compliments which are priceless to me and which, I suppose, cost her nothing. Besides, most people nowadays are so very hard up that I find it delightful to be paid anything."

Mrs. Leverson broke in. "Oscar, you sound—somehow— uncharacteristically sombre. Why so?"

"Ah, Sphinx! Half the world don't believe in God, and the rest don't believe in me."

"That's because you always seem so improbable!" said Ernest Leverson dryly. "You must not be too hard on the world if they take you at your word."

"Ernest, it's always advisable to be at least a little improbable. It affords one a useful point of vantage." He paused, then turned to Ada Leverson. "Sphinx, have I ever told you of how

Jesus came to the terrible realisation that all his efforts had been a waste of time?"

"Is that in the Gospels, Oscar?"

"Not precisely. Scripture loses something in translation."

"Well, in case you *have* told me, tell me again."

Wilde's face assumed a serious expression, and he slowly rose from his chair. Moving nearer Mrs. Leverson, who sat next to Reggie Turner, Wilde set his beverage on the arm of the latter's chair. As he started to talk, he gestured carelessly and knocked his glass into Turner's lap. Turner jumped up and vigourously brushed the liquid from his clothing. Mrs. Leverson fetched a towel which she gave to Turner, who, after he had finished mopping his clothing and then the chair, moved to another chair. Ada prepared and gave Wilde another drink which he received with thanks and apologies. He looked guiltily at Turner and said, "Reggie, I'm so sorry. I ought first to have asked whether you like hock and seltzer."

"Oscar, think nothing of it. I like it, though it's much better as a beverage!"

Wilde laughed heartily, took a sip of his own, and exclaimed, "Yes, indeed!" He set it back down on the same arm of the now-deserted chair. After a short pause he began his parable:

"Christ came to the city and heard the sounds of great rejoicing. He entered a dwelling and saw a man lying drunk upon a couch. He touched him on the shoulder and asked, 'Why do you waste your soul in drink?' The man looked up and answered, 'I was a leper once, and you healed me. What else should I do?' Jesus went further into the city and saw a youth following a harlot, and said to him, 'Why do you look at this woman with eyes of lust?' The youth knew him, and answered, 'I was blind once, and you gave me sight. At what else should I look?' So, he spoke to the woman, 'Why do you walk in the way of sin?' And the woman replied, 'You forgave my sins, and the way is pleasant.' And he passed out of the city and saw an old man weeping by the wayside, and asked him why he wept. The old man answered, 'Lord, I was dead, and you brought me back to life. What else should I do but weep?'"

Everyone was quiet as Wilde ended his apologue, which he did with a sweeping gesture that knocked the second glass into the same, but now-unoccupied, chair. Seeing what he had done, Wilde exclaimed, "Oh, what a waste! I thought Reggie was still sitting there!"

Amid the ensuing laughter, Ada Leverson sprang up and exclaimed, "Next time I must remind everyone that proper dress for these occasions includes mackintoshes!" As she mopped the chair again, she asked, "Oscar, why do you think Jesus considered himself a failure?"

"Ah, I didn't mean that he thought himself a failure, Sphinx," said Wilde as he moved to an ottoman near his hostess. "I said it dawned on him that all his previous efforts had been to no avail. His many miracles amounted to scarcely more than a magician's conjuring and sleight of hand, and his keen insights were merely pearls before swine. He had cheapened his great mission with unworthy toys and baubles to dazzle undiscriminating masses. Jesus was, after all, not only a supreme artist but also a perceptive man who knew that what mankind needed was *not* creeds—they already had far too many—but civilised instincts and imagination. The old religions had imposed silly, arbitrary systems concocted by others. Such rules became obligatory for everyone, despite humankind's primary need for enlightened *self*-realisation, which is the supreme sacrament." Wilde looked around at the others, beamed broadly, and exclaimed, "Here endeth the lesson!"

Ross glanced at his watch. "Oscar, it's quite late!"

"Yes, Robbie, it usually is!" said Wilde softly as he stood. "I can say with Richard the Second, 'I wasted time, and now doth time waste me!'" With a smile to his hosts he said, "Ernest, Sphinx, you are both most kind and hospitable; but there really is more work that I have to do before I return home. And Robbie and Reggie have kindly offered to help me find ways to avoid doing it." Wilde waved at Shannon and Ricketts and expressed the hope that they would invite him to another of their suppers of beer and eggs. "And all of you, my dear friends, will not disappoint me Thursday night. The usual complimentary tickets will be waiting for the four of you at the theatre."

Wilde began to leave, then stopped and turned toward Ada. "My dear Sphinx, I know that Matthew Arnold says he composed the lines in Kensington Gardens, but I'm sure he was thinking of your home when he wrote:

'Calm soul of all things! Make it mine
To feel, amid the city's jar,
That there abides a place of thine,
Man did not make, and can not mar.'"

Then, with just a hint of weariness, Wilde looked over at Ross and Turner. "And now, my friends, shall we exchange this delightful haven for the city's great maw?"

The three men left the Leversons' home and hired a cab, which Wilde entered slowly, followed by Ross and Turner. Upon the cabbie's question about destination, Wilde turned to

Ross. "Robbie, may we go to your home? We wouldn't be able to talk freely in Tite Street."

"Of course, though I don't think I have any wine that's remarkable, or even pretentious."

"Let not your heart be troubled, Robbie; I'm always satisfied by the best." He asked the driver to go to Phillimore Gardens. To Turner, he said, "Reggie, I hope this is satisfactory with you?"

"Yes, indeed. The best wine is also quite satisfactory to me; but after two or three glasses I generally cease being concerned about vintage." Turner laughed and added, "My real preference is for whatever anyone else is buying."

"Reggie," said Wilde, "you should always choose your wines as carefully as you do your friends!"

"And how do you choose your enemies, Oscar?"

"Oh, I don't have to worry about that, Reggie. They choose me!"

At Ross's home the three men discussed Robbie's visit to Sherlock Holmes. Ross explained all that had been said, including Holmes's apparent disinclination at first to accept the invitations. Wilde wondered at that, and heard Ross suggest that it was probably the word *mystery* that had fetched the famous detective.

"Mystery, indeed!" exclaimed Wilde. "But I'm certain that the monstrous Marquess of Queensberry is at the bottom of it." After a pause he added, "And he *is* a monster—without being a myth, which is rather unfair."

Reggie chuckled and said, "Oscar, I like that! I think you ought to use it in one of your plays."

Wilde assured him that he had just recently done so. "And my dear Robbie, you did hear Mr. Holmes say that he and Dr. Watson would be at Kettner's for dinner tomorrow night at eight?"

"Yes."

"And that they will attend my play the next night?"

"Yes. Mr. Holmes said that you'd receive his formal acceptance of both your invitations."

Wilde nodded. "It's perhaps at my home now. I shall have the theatre hold two reserved seats for them." He asked Ross whether Holmes and Watson had seen his first two comedies.

"They both assured me that they had and that they enjoyed them immensely."

Turner spoke up: "Oscar, you'll perhaps be amused to learn that just today I heard a critic from *The Theatre* dismiss *Dorian Gray* and your comedies as nothing more than vehicles for your conversation."

"Everything that I write," said Wilde, "is dominated by my personality. He might as well complain that my sons resemble me."

"Well," observed Ross, "as we three have often agreed, there simply are few *real* critics."

"*Real* critics!" exclaimed Wilde. "How delightfully novel they would be! A silent school of them would be most charming!" He smiled at the prospect. "But, after all is said and done..." He stopped, shook his head, and laughed. "After all is said and done, there's nothing left to say and do, is there?"

Chapter 2

Holmes and Watson arrived at Kettner's a few minutes before eight. They explained to a waiter who their host was and were immediately taken to a private dining area. There they found Robert Ross and his companion, a tall and somewhat portly man whom Watson and Holmes recognized as someone they had seen once or twice but had never met formally. Both Wilde and Ross were impeccably dressed, and Watson was thankful that he had aimed at caution. He decided that Holmes was passable. Wilde and Ross rose as their guests entered.

"My dear Mr. Holmes and Dr. Watson!" exclaimed Wilde. "How good of you both to accept my invitation! I'm Oscar Wilde, and I believe you already know Robbie."

"Yes, indeed," said Holmes, "we enjoyed his company in Baker Street yesterday morning. It's a pleasure to see you again, Mr. Ross."

The two guests found their host to be a man who would have commanded attention in any gathering, and he seemed to know that and to employ speech and gestures to that end. Despite his excess weight, he wore his clothes to good advantage. His attire was of the latest style and a product of the city's most skilled tailors. The flower in his buttonhole and the scarab ring he wore were as much a part of his personality as was his epigrammatic manner of speaking. His cravat was knotted with consummate care, as though to illustrate his aphorism that a well-tied necktie is a man's first serious step in life. Perhaps the only negative feature in his appearance was a noticeable discolouration of his teeth. Wilde was conscious of this and often put his hand before his mouth when he laughed.

After observing the appropriate courtesies, the four men seated themselves. Waiters took their choices, and Wilde ordered wine for everyone. While their dinners were being prepared, the four engaged in small talk. Wilde immediately became aware that Holmes was not much given to idle conversation, and he set upon his task to draw him out. Like almost everyone else who knew Oscar Wilde, Sherlock Holmes later had to admit to being astounded at his host's conversational virtuosity and the breadth of his knowledge. Holmes soon found himself in the midst of a most pleasant duel of wit. There came a point where he was resigned to being out-classed, and delighted to have it so. Almost at once he was content simply to enjoy this new experience that was enhanced by the excellent wine. The matter of Wilde's "mystery" was temporarily forgotten.

Wilde lifted his glass as though in a toast to his three companions. "Gentlemen, this wine upholds admirably the best traditions of Italian winemaking."

Watson sipped his own wine and said, "Yes, it certainly is excellent. But how would you say it compares with French wines?"

"Oh, the Gauls learned winemaking from the Romans. The Italian soils were, and are, ideal for producing wine of the best quality."

To Holmes's assertion that he often found a good glass of Scotch whisky much more effective, Wilde said, "Yes, if one is creating a society of bishops, elders, and censors. But it took the world's *best* wines to produce the Renaissance."

"And the Inquisition?" asked Watson.

"Ah, the Inquisition! For that we can thank the bad fortune that the popes who authorized it, while perhaps quite free from error on dogma, knew nothing of vintages."

"Oscar," exclaimed Ross, "I've never heard this before, even though I'm a Catholic! Is it a fact?"

Wilde laughed. "Well, if it isn't, it ought to be." He paused and looked chidingly at Ross. "Robbie, you must not worship facts. That is *not* in the catechism."

"But, Oscar," said Ross, "I've heard you heap great praise on the French."

"Of course, Robbie, when I speak of their literature. French prose is perfect. But, unfortunately, since most people read nothing but newspapers, French literature, like most other nations' literatures, has little effect outside an educated minority. And the difference between literature and newspapers is that newspapers are unreadable and literature is not read."

Watson spoke up: "Mr. Wilde, you said something about a society of bishops and elders. I assume that you are not an admirer of organised religion."

Wilde shook his head. "No, I prefer that all human endeavour be unorganised, that is, that it be free of outside interference. It serves an individual badly to turn him into an imitation of someone else, in whatever area. Mankind's progress has come through those rare persons who have refused to be organised."

Holmes nodded vigourously. "And of course, this applies to religious beliefs."

"Especially to religious beliefs," replied Wilde. "Unfortunately, almost all religious organisers have had little sense of style and absolutely no appreciation of individuality. A formalised creed may be useful up to the age of five or six, as an accompaniment perhaps of the great fairy tales. Thereafter, a creed becomes tiresome and meaningless and, carried into adulthood, usually produces only Tartuffes and Pecksniffs. Even the delightful words of Jesus, repeated too often and in an uninspired way, tend to become a bore. But can you imagine how powerful an effect they would have if a young person first encountered them when on the threshold of adulthood?" Wilde reached out and patted Ross's arm. "Now, Robbie, nothing that I say here is intended to diminish your love of Holy Church."

"Oh, I know that, Oscar. Besides, I spend much of my time praying for your conversion!"

"Robbie, you are incorrigible!" exclaimed Wilde with a hearty laugh. "Ah, prayer! This may come as a great surprise to you, Robbie: I admire prayer and grant that it has much importance. Everyone should pray."

"Really?" said Holmes.

"Oh, indeed! However, one should never expect prayer to be answered. Otherwise, it ceases to be prayer and becomes conversation. Prayer is a special privilege, but it would be utterly presumptuous of us to expect our childish wishes to be gratified. Analyse the *Our Father*, the only paradigm for praying that Jesus gave us, and you will see that, except a few intangible generalities, it asks for only one simple item—food. And even that is requested only for the present. 'Give us *this* day,' and so on. This small concession was simply Jesus' realisation that he could not leave his untutored followers without at least a token item to pray for."

Wilde's conversation was, to many, almost mesmerising. In referring to him, the word *conversation* was barely appropriate; for he sooner or later dominated whatever group he was in, not because he imposed himself but rather because everyone else was content simply to hear him talk. His voice seemed especially suited to commanding attention, and his speech was as beautifully crafted as was his writing. He enjoyed using certain words, almost as though he could taste them. Such words as *crimson, charming*, and *tedious* fell from his lips as the tones from a fine violin in the hands of a master. He might have been describing his own conversation when, in *The Picture of Dorian Gray*, he wrote of Lord Henry Wotton :

> He played with the idea, and grew wilful; tossed it into the air and transformed it; let it escape and recaptured it; made it iridescent with fancy and winged it with paradox. The praise of folly, as he went on, soared into a philosophy, and Philosophy herself became young, and catching the mad music of Pleasure, wearing, one might fancy, her wine-stained robe and wreath of ivy, danced like a Bacchante over the hills of life, and mocked the slow Silenus for being sober. Facts fled before her like frightened forest things....

Holmes said, "Mr. Wilde, I remember attending a performance about fourteen years ago of Messrs. Gilbert and Sullivan's operetta *Patience*. I was amused by it at the time, but I have often wondered what you thought of their caricature of your advocacy of aesthetics and the idea of 'art for art's sake.'"

"Oh," laughed Wilde, "that was very well done—a capital spoof. I told them so at the time. And it gave Mr. D'Oyly Carte the idea to send me to America for a delightful year of lecturing, a living advertisement for the operetta."

Watson chuckled and quoted:

"'Though the Philistines may jostle, you will rank as an apostle in the high aesthetic band,
If you walk down Piccadilly with a poppy or a lily in your mediaeval hand.'

Did you really do that, Mr. Wilde?"

"Oh, no, Dr. Watson, but I made the world *think* I had done it, which is much more difficult." With a shake of his head Wilde added: "I don't believe the Americans have ever forgiven me, however, for suggesting that there were things they needed to learn. Indeed they did not understand, and still cannot, that real art does not serve any *practical* end. It is quite useless and justifies itself simply by existing." He looked somber and almost whispered, "I did not tell them of my fear that the discovery of America was the beginning of the death of art."

Watson broke in quickly: "Mr. Wilde, have you ever considered collaborating with someone, as Gilbert and Sullivan have done?"

"Oh, no!"

"Why not, Oscar?" asked Ross.

"My dear Robbie, an artist moves in a cycle of masterpieces, and that cycle is not made for two." This amused the group, with Wilde laughing as heartily as the others.

Wilde extended a hand toward Watson and exclaimed: "But, Dr. Watson, you yourself have produced some very admirable work in your chronicles of Mr. Holmes's fascinating exploits. I was particularly taken by *A Study in Scarlet*, some years back."

"Ah, *that* one!" said Watson with a chuckle. "I had grown weary of trying to find a publisher for it, and Ward, Lock and Company accepted it. But I wasn't very happy with them. I made the mistake of giving up all proprietary rights to it."

"Yes, I had my own problems with Ward, Lock," said Wilde. "I let them have *Dorian Gray* for only ten percent. They said nothing more was ever given, but I found out better afterward." He took a sip of wine. "I've been especially enjoying the short pieces you've done more recently for the *Strand*, Dr. Watson. 'The Speckled Band,' for instance was very effective, I thought."

"Thank you," said Watson. "I still become uncomfortable when I recall the situation in which Holmes and I found ourselves during that case. I've never been very comfortable around snakes."

"Mr. Holmes," said Ross, "I was interested by Dr. Watson's description of your confrontation with that murderous fiend, Dr. Grimesby Roylott, right in your home. That must have been especially unnerving."

Wilde broke in with a knowing look at Ross. "Indeed! Mr. Holmes. I could not help being reminded of some of my own special enemies. But you stood up to Roylott admirably."

Watson exclaimed, "I was certainly aghast, Holmes, when Roylott picked up that poker, and relieved when all he did was, with childish bravado, to bend it."

"Oh, he was quite a bully," said Holmes. "And while I did not wish to destroy any of our furniture, or disturb our landlady, I think I might have held my own with him. I've had some success with the martial arts, including both jujitsu and tae-kwon-do."

Watson shook his head sadly. "The newspapers' reporting of that entire case was totally inadequate."

"Well," said Wilde, "your own accounts entirely make up for the journalists' failure. I fear that the press are our modern alchemists. They turn even the most precious stories into the basest prose."

Holmes shook his head. "In the reporting of technical matters, I find myself more on the side of the newspapers, except, of course, when they misstate facts."

"Well," observed Wilde, "one might forgive them even that, if their misstatements were artistically imaginative. But more often than not journalism exhibits ineptness made tedious by moralising."

"Yes," said Watson with a wry glance at Holmes, "My friend here tells me that I always sensationalise his cases."

"You *do*, my dear fellow. If my work has any value at all, it is in my advocacy of the value of careful observation and logical deduction. I must, of course, admit to being flattered by your obvious admiration; but I think one must not lose sight of the greater purpose."

Wilde quickly took up the matter. "Mr. Holmes, why don't you write up some of your cases as you believe they should be done?"

"I have every intention of doing so."

"But when will that be?"

"I've asked him the same question," said Watson.

After they had dined and while they sipped their port, some further general conversation ensued until Holmes observed: "Mr. Wilde, as much as I am enjoying our conversation, I know that you brought me here to explain a problem that you are having and with which you wish my assistance." Even as Holmes introduced the subject, Watson took out his tablet and prepared to take notes during the discussion.

Wilde's face assumed a serious expression. He reached inside his coat and brought out an envelope containing a four-by-six-inch photograph. This he handed to Holmes, who examined it and passed it to Watson, remarking as he did so that it appeared to be a photograph of a painting of Wilde.

Wilde produced another photograph and handed it to Holmes, who glanced at it and, with a nod, said, "Yes, this appears to be a duplicate." He started to pass the second one to Watson but stopped and looked again more closely. "No, they aren't quite the same. Interesting!"

Wilde brought out seven more envelopes, each of which contained a photograph, and handed them to Holmes. The detective stacked them on the table, as one would playing cards. "I count nine."

"Examine them carefully," said Wilde softly, "in the order that I handed them to you. You'll notice successive alterations. I've written on the back of each photograph the date of its posting."

Holmes laid them out separately on the table in chronological order. He then picked up the first in one hand and the latest in the other, and compared the two. "Aha! Yes, I now see clearly what you mean." He then reexamined all the others. The face in particular was undergoing a transformation. In the eighth and ninth photographs the ears appeared to suggest those of a satyr, and around the eyes there was the beginning of a leer. The effect was heightened, and made strangely sinister, by the altered mouth. All of it was subtle but undeniable. The figure's clothing was changing, too, though less dramatically. "They aren't identical," murmured Holmes. "Each is slightly different."

"Exactly, Mr. Holmes," said Wilde. "Are you familiar with my novel, *The Picture of Dorian Gray?*"

"I know that you wrote the book, though I haven't read it. Watson, I believe you've read it?"

"Yes, I have. A clever and beautifully written story, and very witty."

Holmes asked where the photographs had come from.

"That's what I was hoping you might help me discover."

"Have you any theories?"

Wilde nodded. "Yes, but nothing concrete to fix suspicion on any one person." After a pause he added, "But there is one whom I consider the most likely person—John Sholto Douglas, Marquess of Queensberry."

Holmes glanced at Watson, and nodded. "We're somewhat familiar with him. Why do you name him?"

"Because I've already had difficulties with him and found him quite mad. His youngest son, Lord Alfred, is a close friend of mine; and the scarlet, screaming marquess cannot tolerate that. He has alienated every member of his family and grossly insulted his wife, who had to divorce him. He has also insulted many others who have disagreed with him."

"Much of this is familiar to me," said Holmes. "Also, as an amateur pugilist, I am aware of the Queensberry rules of boxing. Do you have other suspects?"

"No one of the same character as Queensberry. Oh, there are two actors in London who certainly waste no opportunity to express their dislike, but I don't think they would be likely to pursue me in this melodramatic way."

"Nevertheless, who are they?"

· "Charles Hawtrey and Charles Brookfield."

Holmes looked over at Watson. "Are you getting all this down?" Watson nodded as he wrote the last bit of information. Holmes looked keenly at Wilde and asked, "Do any of these individuals you've mentioned have artistic ability? That is, could any of them paint such a portrait?" He picked up one of the photos and looked at it. "Though this photograph probably reduces the picture greatly, it clearly indicates more than amateur ability."

Wilde shook his head. "I know of no such ability in any of them. Of course, any one of them might have hired some artist to do the work."

"Of course," said Holmes. "Oh, one other thing, Mr. Wilde: When did you receive the first photograph?"

"Eleven days ago."

"And the most recent?"

"Today. Except for two days, I've received one every day, all of them postmarked London."

"I'll need to examine carefully both the photographs and the envelopes. May I take them with me?"

"Of course," said Wilde as he handed them to Holmes, "but I suspect that I haven't received the last one."

"Why do you think so?"

"Well, Mr. Holmes, if the sender intends to mimic the portrait in my book, he has a considerable amount of work yet to do. Dorian Gray's portrait was altered quite beyond recognition."

"Indeed! Well, I depend upon you to furnish me with all the photographs you may get, their envelopes, and anything else that seems even remotely connected with this. Even the merest detail."

"I shall certainly do so, Mr. Holmes." He sighed. "It is indeed a bore to be harassed by such childish games."

Holmes rose and the other three did also. After accepting Wilde's visiting card, Holmes said: "And Mr. Wilde, if this is the greatest problem that troubles you, I think we may certainly expect soon, without great ado, to relieve any anxiety you may have. This matter does not seem to be a complex one, though it is not without interest. I shall let you know as soon as I think I have anything of substance to tell you. In the meantime, let me know if any crisis arises. And thank you for a very pleasant evening."

"I thank you, too, Mr. Wilde," said Watson, "and a good evening to you, Mr. Ross."

"Remember," Wilde exclaimed , "tomorrow evening—at the Haymarket! I hope to see you both at the first night of *An Ideal Husband*. The title, of course, is ironic, as are most husbands. Marriage! It's main charm is that it makes a life of deception absolutely necessary." He smiled and added, "Being successful in marriage and writing a good comedy! Each requires a taste for irony and a sense of the ridiculous."

"Well," said Holmes, "that I would not know. The fair sex are Dr. Watson's domain. I wish you both a good evening!"

Wilde and Ross returned to their seats and discussed their recent guests. Dr. Watson struck them as a civilised, pleasant, uncomplicated fellow who was obviously overshadowed by Sherlock Holmes and, apparently, comfortable in that role. Holmes, however, was quite another matter. Ross thought him obsessive and willful, and he saw serious gaps in the detective's interests.

Wilde agreed but suggested that Holmes combined fierce determination with great intelligence. "And that's exactly what we want, isn't it, Robbie?" After a moment of silence he nodded and said, "I do believe that we have found the right person. And if Queensberry is indeed at the bottom of this, it will be a capital show to observe how Holmes deals with him. Already I feel much relieved."

After enjoying a moment of calm repose, the two men rose and Wilde said brightly: "Well, Robbie, I have a busy day tomorrow, even before getting to the theatre." He paused, then added, "I've heard that the infamous marquess is threatening to do something to disrupt the first night." To Ross's question as to whether Herbert Tree had been warned, Wilde replied that Tree was in America but that others seemed to be taking sufficient precautions in cooperation with the police. And since the Prince of Wales intended to be present, those precautions assumed special importance.

Wilde quickly changed the subject: "Oh, I forgot to tell you that Brendan Halbert has asked to interview me for *Sketch*, so I'll have to work that in somewhere after tomorrow night. I don't wish the critics to think I've forgotten them."

Ross nodded. "I don't think Halbert's for sale as I've heard a lot of other critics are."

"For sale, indeed," replied Wilde, "but one gathers that they cannot be very expensive."

Both men left the restaurant and walked slowly to the street. Wilde signalled to a hansom which stopped and allowed the two men to enter. A passing couple were having difficulty with their young son, who was crying piteously. Wilde observed him solemnly and murmured, "So young and already so disillusioned!"

For eight years Herbert Beerbohm Tree had been the very successful and respected actor-manager of the Haymarket Theatre. Compared with George Alexander, actor-manager at the St. James's Theatre, Tree was the more versatile actor. Tree admired Wilde's ability to write sparkling dialogue, seemingly without effort. When in 1893 he played the role of Lord Illingworth in Wilde's *A Woman of No Importance*, Tree was so much affected by Illingworth's witty lines that the actor subsequently almost developed a new personality. Many agreed that, at the very least, it had altered Tree's conversation. Even Wilde commented about it: "Ah, every day dear Herbert becomes more and more Oscarised. It is a wonderful case of Nature imitating Art."

After Tree's successful first night as Lord Illingworth, Wilde had gone backstage and exclaimed to him, "I shall always regard you as the best critic of my plays."

"But," replied Tree, "I have never criticised your plays."

"Yes, and that's why."

Tree had been aware for some months that Wilde was having problems, though he had no conception of the seriousness and the extent of those problems. Earlier Tree had received a copy, anonymously delivered, of a very personal letter that Wilde had written to Alfred Douglas. It was sent to Tree in order to convince Wilde of the earnestness of the blackmailers' demands. Sensing the possibly damaging effect the letter might have in hostile hands, Tree mentioned it to Wilde.

As he handed the copy to Wilde, Tree remarked that the phrasing might be misconstrued; but Wilde explained that it was a prose poem with fanciful allusions and that, if put into verse form, it might be printed in a respected anthology of poetry.

"Yes, but it isn't in verse."

"That," countered Wilde, "doubtless explains why it isn't in an anthology of poetry."

To prevent any untoward event, the theatre requested help from the police to deter Queensberry or anyone else on the outside from creating a disturbance on the first night of *An Ideal Husband*. It is also quite possible that the Prince of Wales, an admirer of Wilde's literary accomplishments, used his influence. Nevertheless, among the theatre's regular actors there were two of Wilde's bitterest enemies, and both were in the cast. Charles H. Hawtrey was to play Lord Goring, the most entertaining role and the one that had much of Wilde himself in it. The other was Charles H. Brookfield, who had long detested Wilde. During the rehearsals the playwright provided Brookfield with yet another irritant. Wilde had rather uncharitably insisted that the cast rehearse on Christmas Day, and Brookfield was furious.

"Don't you keep Christmas, Oscar?"

"No, Brookfield, the only festival of the Church I keep is Septuagesima. Do you keep Septuagesima, Brookfield?"

"Not since I was a boy."

"Ah, be a boy again!"

Early in the afternoon before *An Ideal Husband* opened at the Haymarket, a young man accosted Wilde as he was leaving his home to go to the theatre.

"Mr. Wilde?"

"Yes. Who are you?"

"Allen, Mr. Wilde. I'm here to offer you first chance to buy one of your letters."

"What letter?" Allen handed it to him, and Wilde quickly saw that it was the original of the copy which he and Tree had discussed earlier. "And may I ask what price you put on it?"

"Ten pounds."

"Ten pounds!" exclaimed Wilde. "You have no appreciation of literature. If you had asked me for fifty pounds, I might have given it to you. I look upon it as a work of art." He handed it back to Allen and said, "But don't trouble yourself, for Mr. Tree has given me a copy of that letter. The original is of no use to me. Goodnight!"

A few minutes later, just outside the Haymarket's stage door, Wilde was approached by another young man. "And who are you?" asked Wilde.

"That ain't important, sir. What's important is these here letters you wrote to Lord Alfred. Would you like to have 'em?"

"If they are all as perfect as the one of which some kind person sent a copy to Mr. Tree, I should certainly like to have them. But why not continue your admirable practice of sending copies? Then I should not need the originals."

"How much will you give for 'em?"

"One cannot estimate their value in money. The price of beauty is above rubies."

"Well," said the young man encouragingly, "you can have 'em for thirty quid."

"Why do you want thirty pounds?"

"I want to go to America and make a fresh start."

"A strange design," said Wilde, "but not—if you will pardon the reflection—not original. Columbus thought of it before you. I hope you will be more fortunate than he, and miss the continent on your way." Wilde wrote a cheque for thirty pounds and handed it to the man. "Now, goodbye. The best advice I can give you is that on the day you land in America, you set sail for England." The man left and Wilde, after glancing through the letters, saw at once that the one Allen had offered earlier was not among them.

Later that afternoon, as Wilde started to enter his home, the first blackmailer, Allen, called to him and offered the earlier, missing letter. Wilde repeated his previous refusal to purchase it, and the blackmailer said, "A curious construction could be put on that letter."

"Art is seldom intelligible to the criminal classes," said Wilde.

"A man has offered me sixty pounds for it."

"If you take my advice," said Wilde, "you will go to him at once and sell it. I myself have never received so large a sum for any prose work of that length."

"The man is out of town."

"He will come back, and I assure you on my word of honor that I shall pay nothing for that letter."

The man whined that he was penniless, that he needed help.

"Well," said Wilde, "I can't guarantee your cab expenses, but here's a half-sovereign. Now, please excuse me."

About an hour later, another member of the gang appeared at Wilde's door. Wilde was furious. "I can't be bothered any more about that letter! I don't care tuppence about it!"

"But, sir, Dennis Cassidy told me to give the letter back to you."

A surprised Wilde exclaimed, "Give it back? Why?"

"Well, he says that you were kind to him, and that there's no use trying to rent you, as you only laugh at us."

Wilde glanced at the soiled, much-handled letter. "I think it quite unpardonable that better care was not taken of an original work of mine." As he took ten shillings from his pocket and handed it to the man, he said, "I'm afraid you are leading a wonderfully wicked life."

"There's good and bad in every one of us."

"You are a born philosopher," said Wilde. "Good night."

Sherlock Holmes and John Watson arrived in front of the theatre about a quarter-hour before the play was to start. They entered and immediately saw Lewis Waller, who was in charge while Tree was absent in America. He gave them their tickets and commented that he remembered seeing both men once or twice. He assured them he was honored by their presence. "Mr. Wilde said I should expect you, and I hope you will let me know if there is anything our house may do for you. We're assuming that tonight will make a trio of the already-sparkling pair of Mr. Wilde's comedies."

"Yes, indeed," exclaimed Watson, "if this is comparable to the first two plays, all of you are to be congratulated!"

Holmes asked Waller whether it might be possible to step backstage after the performance; and the theatre manager exclaimed that of course he should, and that Wilde had already explained Holmes's wish to do that. "I believe," added Waller, "you may also expect to see the Prince of Wales. Whenever he attends, he usually asks to go back to thank the cast and staff."

"Indeed! How democratic!" exclaimed Holmes with an arch glance at Watson. "And now, we won't impose on you further, Mr. Waller." The three men shook hands and parted.

As Holmes and Watson glanced about the lobby, they saw a number of policemen, most of whom they recognised and nodded to. Holmes saw one officer in particular and walked over to him. "Tobias Gregson! The smartest of the Scotland Yarders!"

"Mr. Holmes! Good evening, sir! Well, we are watching out for anyone who might be trying to cause any trouble."

"Then, I should think anyone trying to cause trouble had better beware! You're the Yard's best bulldog."

"I thank you, sir. Well, I'd better be at my duty or you'll be calling me your favourite tabby cat"

Wilde entered the lobby and sauntered over to them. "Mr. Holmes! Dr. Watson! How delightful to see you again. I hope you won't be upset that you'll be seated with Mrs. Wilde and me."

"It will be an honour," said Watson. As they arrived at their seats, Watson was much taken by Constance Wilde's beauty and the attractiveness of her attire. Wilde introduced his two guests to her, and they sat with Mrs. Wilde between them and her husband. Since he was sitting next to Constance Wilde, Watson engaged her in a brief exchange. While she apparently took immediately to Watson, both Holmes and Watson thought they detected in her a reluctance to be present.

The play was acted beautifully and received great applause. Some critics, however, were captious in later comments, one of them suggesting lack of originality, and that as the previous comedy had been tinged with "the colouring of the Norwegian school," *An Ideal Husband* showed the influence of French playwrights Augustin Scribe and Victorien Sardou. But any doubters in the audience were few and, apparently, in camouflage. Continued applause and cries for the author filled the auditorium. Holmes and Watson looked at Wilde, but the latter leaned over and said softly, "One cannot afford to exhibit oneself too often before an audience. Otherwise, one begins to feel like the bird in a cuckoo clock." Nevertheless, Wilde somewhat reluctantly went to the stage, his bows accompanied by increased and loud acclaim. After Wilde rejoined his wife and guests, the four made their way through the many well-wishers and finally arrived backstage.

They at once observed a small crowd of actors and stage-hands gathered around the Prince of Wales. As the Wildes and their two guests appeared, the prince strode over and expressed to Wilde his congratulations upon the play's wonderful and well-deserved reception.

"Thank you, Your Highness. Yes, the audience were a great success tonight! I felt that it was they who should have been called before the footlights."

"Well," said Prince Edward, "second only to the author's success."

Wilde smiled and explained that the play was too long and needed some deletions. The Prince shook his head. "I say emphatically, pray do not take out a single word!"

Wilde's face registered his pleasure. "You are most kind, Prince Edward. And no one ever appealed in vain to my laziness."

The following day Wilde, in the study of his Tite Street home, was interviewed by Brendan Halbert for an article the latter was writing for the periodical *Sketch*. While Wilde smoked one of his gold-tipped cigarettes, he and Halbert spent the first several minutes on mostly general matters. Then the journalist, after citing several critical reviews of the new play, asked, "Mr. Wilde, how would you define ideal dramatic criticism?"

"As far as my work is concerned?"

"Yes."

"Unqualified appreciation."

This brought a broad grin from the interviewer, who then asked whether Wilde had seen Bernard Shaw's comments about the new play.

"Not yet, though his reviews of my two previous plays were most perceptive."

"He praised them highly, I believe," said Halbert.

"Yes, that's what I meant."

Halbert picked up a paper and read from Shaw's latest commentary: "'Mr. Oscar Wilde's new play at the Haymarket is a dangerous subject, because he has the property of making his critics dull. They laugh angrily at his epigrams, like a child who is coaxed into being amused in the very act of setting up a yell of rage and agony.'"

"Exactly," said Wilde. "And Mr. Shaw has succinctly explained how foolish it is for a man to represent himself as a dramatic critic. It would be as silly as pretending to be a critic of epics or a pastoral critic or a critic of lyrics. The aim of the true critic is to try to chronicle his own moods, not to try to correct the masterpieces of others."

"But don't you wish to please the critics?" asked the interviewer.

Wilde tapped the ash from his cigarette and took a long puff on it. "I do not write to please cliques." He chuckled and said, " No, indeed; I write to please myself. And I never reply to critics; I'll save all that for my dotage."

"Well, Mr. Wilde, when you present a new play, what sort of reaction do you hope to get from the public?"

"Which public? There are as many publics as there are personalities."

"But," persisted Halbert, "how do you feel just before the curtain opens on a first night?"

"I am exquisitely indifferent. I know after the last dress rehearsal what effect my play has produced upon me, and my interest in the play ends there. I then feel curiously envious of the public; they have such wonderfully fresh emotions in store for them."

"But even that," said Halbert, "can't insure a play's success."

Wilde smiled and took a puff on his cigarette. "The real question at that point is whether the *audience* will be a success, and on the three first nights I've had in London the public have performed beautifully."

"Mr. Wilde, I understand that your fourth play is nearly completed."

"Yes, I believe Mr. Alexander expects *The Importance of Being Earnest* to open sometime in February."

"Do you think the critics will understand it?"

"I hope not."

Halbert chuckled. "What sort of play are we to expect?"

"It is exquisitely trivial, a delicate bubble of fancy. And it has its philosophy."

"Its philosophy?"

"Yes, that we should treat all the trivial things of life seriously, and all the serious things of life with sincere and studied triviality."

"But, Mr. Wilde, how would our present British society be able to continue by using that philosophy?"

"It couldn't, and therein lies its usefulness."

After recovering from uproarious laughter, Halbert asked whether Wilde had worked out any ideas for his next play.

"Nothing definite yet, but I think I might like to write a play about modern marriage."

"Something like *An Ideal Husband?*"

"No, I see something more like a story by M. de Maupassant—bitter and ironic."

"And amusing?" asked Halbert.

"Inevitably; it involves marriage. I see a young couple who marry for all the wrong reasons, and then decide to stay together, also for all the wrong reasons. But it ends happily."

"They work out their problems?"

"Oh, yes. In fact, it becomes an idyllic marriage, with a fairy tale ending. They are at last divorced and live happily ever after."

Halbert smiled as he laid his notebook aside. "But one thing still bothers me, Mr. Wilde."

"Only one? My dear fellow, how do you produce anything of substance? Epictetus very perceptively assures us that difficulties define character."

Halbert smiled and said modestly, "Perhaps I'm *not* very productive." He paused as though trying to frame his question precisely. "But, Mr. Wilde, I get the impression that you think the press is your enemy."

"Oh, no, not an enemy, but certainly often lacking in imagination. I still recall the childish suggestion by the *St. James's Gazette* that *The Picture of Dorian Gray* should be 'chucked into the fire.' I felt it necessary to remind them that this is what one does with newspapers."

"Well, sir, let's get a bit closer to the matter. What is your main complaint about journalists?"

"My *main* complaint!" exclaimed Wilde. "Ah! Several contend for precedence. But I suppose I'd say that the journalist almost always misses the point of art. Too often he seems to think that art must be popular, even though it is the public that should try to be artistic. Too often he insists that art must inculcate morality—his own ideas of morality, of course. But neither morality nor immorality should be an issue for the artist."

"Yes," said Halbert, "I recall something in your preface to *Dorian Gray*—'There is no such thing as a moral or an immoral book. Books are well written or badly written.' Do you still hold that?"

"Of course. And I say also in that preface that what the world calls vice and virtue are both simply raw materials for the artist. A true artist can express everything; he is articulate on many subjects."

Halbert nodded. "Yes, I can see that. What else? You said you had several complaints."

Wilde discarded his cigarette in an ashtray and replied slyly: "The journalist insists on reminding the public of the existence of the artist, which is unnecessary. He is always reminding the artist of the existence of the public. *That* is indecent."

With a twinkle in his eye Halbert thanked Wilde for granting the interview.

"You're quite welcome; it has been a pleasure. I'm sure that you must have a great future in literature."

Halbert smiled broadly and asked why he thought so.

"Because you seem to be such a very bad interviewer. I feel sure that you must write poetry. I certainly like the colour of your necktie very much."

Chapter 3

Sherlock Holmes stood before the fireplace, apparently deep in thought. Watson reached into a box of cigars, selected one, and proceeded to remove its tip with his penknife. As he started to light it, Holmes abruptly asked: "Well, Watson, which is your favourite modern painter?"

Watson laughed. "I ought to know better than to be surprised by your sudden and very apt questions. Nevertheless, how the dickens did you know I'd been reading about modern painters?"

Holmes smiled and sat down. "By the best of methods, my dear fellow—observation and deduction. Lately our charwoman has been a bit lax with her dusting, and I noticed a definite telltale spot of disturbed dust where our volume on modern artists had stood unexamined for—well, long enough to allow a considerable accrual of Baker Street dust."

"Quite so!" laughed Watson.

"And what conclusions did you reach?" asked Holmes.

"About whom?"

"Oh, whomever you like—Dante Gabriel Rossetti, for instance."

"I suppose I left a bookmark at that place?"

"No, you merely turned down the corner of a page. So, I repeat, what conclusions did you reach?"

Watson shrugged. "Oh, I don't know. Rossetti and his Pre-Raphaelite brotherhood have produced some interesting work, though Rossetti seems to have been undecided which to follow, painting or poetry. In fact, I think he's quoted as saying that if he could have lived by painting, he'd have seen poetry damned. And did you know that he had a dog named Dizzy? Or that *sloshy* was one of his favorite words? Or that he was once chased around his garden by an angry zebu that he was trying to show to Whistler?"

Holmes threw his head back and laughed. "No I did not know all this, and I'm not quite sure how that information would help with Mr. Wilde's case. But you mentioned Whistler. What do you know about him?"

"Oh, the usual sort of thing. He is by birth an American and, oddly, went to their military college at West Point—imagine that! He has lived many years in England and on the Continent. I understand that nowadays when he speaks to Americans, he does it with something of a British accent, and in an American one when speaking to an Englishman. He's very egotistical and talented. I shan't forget his amusing legal encounter with John Ruskin!"

"And how about his more recent feud with our client, Oscar Wilde?"

Watson shook his head. "That I'm not very familiar with. I seem to recall that it wasn't serious."

"Oh, certainly not so serious as amusing. Wilde had become a great admirer of Whistler and was always happy to be seen in his company. And Whistler was quite content to continue this arrangement until the younger man began to develop his own odd, flamboyant, and entertaining personality and views. *That* Whistler could not tolerate, and there was a breach in their relationship."

Watson looked at Holmes inquiringly. "Does this have some bearing on what Wilde has asked you to do?"

"After recalling their somewhat public differences, I wondered whether there might be a connection. I've done some investigating and made a few inquiries." Holmes rose and went over to a box on his desk. From it he retrieved the several photographs that Wilde had given him. "I've examined several of Whistler's paintings here in London, originals or copies, and spoken with a number of people who know him and something of his style of painting. And by the way, he's back in London from a considerable stay in France. That is instructive." Holmes held up one of the copies of the painting of Wilde. "This, for instance, has definite features that might make one suspect Whistler as the artist. I even went over to where Frederick Leyland used to live. As you may know, he died a few years ago; but his Peacock Room, that Whistler created, is still intact."

"Oh," laughed Watson, "I do indeed recall the dispute between Whistler and Leyland. I think the artist was quite outrageous and that Leyland would have been justified in bringing charges."

"Well," said Holmes, "Whistler's little duel with Wilde was quite as animated and public, though there was no money involved." Holmes held up one of the Wilde photos. "There are definite characteristics in this little photograph that I believe

I see in some of Whistler's paintings." Holmes held the picture up for Watson to see. "Compare this with his two *Arrangements in Grey and Black*, the paintings of his mother and of Thomas Carlyle—indeed, even his portrait of Leyland. And notice, for example, his rendering of the folds in the clothing."

"Do you think it conclusive?" asked Watson.

"Perhaps not, but there is even further evidence." Holmes held up the envelopes. "All of these are quite clearly of French manufacture, not surprising since our suspect has been for some time in that country." Holmes then picked out one envelope that was slightly different from the others. "The sender used a different envelope when he sent the fifth photograph; you'll see that neither the texture of the paper nor its colour is the same."

"Is *that* conclusive?"

"Perhaps not by itself," said Holmes, "but there is an interesting little detail on the back of this envelope. Probably in his haste, the artist failed to notice that he was using an envelope that had perhaps been personalised by his stationer. Embossed on its back is a small butterfly."

"Ha! The same butterfly that one often sees as Whistler's signature on works of art. He must have picked up that distinctive envelope without noticing his famous symbol. Why, then, Holmes, you have your case!"

"I think so. If I needed further evidence, I have it in a peculiar little detail in the dates on which these photographs were posted. If you look through them, you will see that there is a gap of two days in their postings, December 28 and 29. And for half a crown I persuaded a cab driver to verify that our Mr. Whistler was absent from London on those two days."

FRED W. EDMISTON —

"Then you've completed your case!" exclaimed Watson. "What's the next step? Will you confront Whistler with this evidence?"

Holmes shook his head. "That really is not our concern. The painter has apparently committed no crime. I shall give all this information to Mr. Wilde and let him decide whether to press the matter. But I'll suggest that he either ignore it entirely, or merely inform Mr. Whistler, by the post or perhaps through a third party, that he is flattered by the painter's interest—that he likes the portrait even if the Royal Academy perhaps do not."

"But Whistler is a very volatile man," said Watson, "and even that might well incite some sort of unfortunate response."

"Mr. Wilde will have to decide that for himself. Besides, from reports I've received, he has far more serious concerns." Holmes got up and put the photographs back into their box. He then picked up his hat and topcoat and walked to the door. Turning back to Watson, he said, "I shall send Mr. Wilde a request to let me call tomorrow morning."

At a few minutes past ten o'clock the following morning, Oscar Wilde stepped outside his home at 16 Tite Street just in time to meet a tax collector.

"Ah, you must be Mr. Wilde!"

"Yes, I must be. No one else wanted the job!"

"Well, sir, I've come to collect your taxes."

"Taxes?" exclaimed Wilde. "Why should I pay taxes?"

"Well, Mr. Wilde, you're the householder. You live here, don't you? Or at least you sleep here, I believe."

"Ah, yes! But then, you see, I sleep so badly."

"I'm sorry for that, Mr. Wilde, but I must nevertheless collect the taxes."

"Oh, very well!" said Wilde with a sigh. "Let me go inside and write you a cheque." The two men entered the house and passed Wilde's young footman in the hall. Wilde explained to him that Constance Wilde and the two boys had gone out several minutes before and would not return until midafternoon at the earliest. He told the footman also that Sherlock Holmes would call shortly and should be admitted. After the footman left, Wilde gave the tax collector his cheque and saw him to the door.

Hardly had Wilde reached his study when there was a knock at the front door. The servant answered it, admitted Holmes, and showed him into the drawing room as instructed. Overhearing the exchange between Holmes and the footman, Wilde returned and entered the room where Holmes had already taken a seat. Upon Wilde's entering, the detective rose and was greeted warmly by Wilde.

"Ah, Mr. Holmes, how good to see you again." Wilde gestured toward the chair Holmes had been sitting in. "Please, please, be seated. And now, do you have good news, or must I continue to wonder?"

"I believe, Mr. Wilde, that we have settled the mystery as to the sender. And if correct, I can say that the sender was also the artist."

Wilde looked surprised. "Do you mean that Queensberry had nothing to do with it?

"I think it improbable." He then gave his reasons and showed Wilde the various items that bore evidence of James Whistler's having sent the photographs.

At the conclusion of Holmes' explanation, Wilde sank slowly back into his chair. With a shake of his head he exclaimed, "How childish of Jimmy!" He took a puff of his cigarette. "I'm greatly in your debt, Mr. Holmes, for the skill and dispatch with which you have done your work. I must say, however, that I'm rather surprised that it was not another silly display of immaturity by the Marquess of Queensberry. I had hoped that any contact between Jimmy Whistler and myself was long over. We haven't met socially for over ten years." He shook his head and added, "I hadn't even heard that he was back in London. I suppose he found the many great painters in France too intolerable." With an expression almost of hopeful expectation Wilde asked, "And you see no evidence that anyone else was involved in the matter?"

"It's unlikely. Therefore, Mr. Wilde, I return your items and say only that you now know the origin of the photographs. What you do with that information is entirely up to you. My advice is that you either ignore it or do nothing more than let Whistler know that he has been found out. This should stop his sending them. I'd suggest nothing stronger than a short note to thank him for his flattering attention." Holmes was aware of his client's serious countenance. "Mr. Wilde, I must say that you appear to be disappointed at my conclusions."

"I have only hinted to you, Mr. Holmes, about my problems with Queensberry. When I told you of the several photographs, I naturally assumed he was responsible for them, and was hopeful that your investigation would confirm it."

"Would it have made much difference if Queensberry had sent them?"

"It would at least have simplified my concern. What you tell me makes my situation more complex."

Holmes remained silent for a moment, then turned to Wilde with the manner of someone who had resolved his own personal dilemma. "Mr. Wilde, I must tell you candidly that I have become aware of some of the problems you have been dealing with. I won't try to explain my sources, but will say merely that my work requires a keen awareness of much that happens in London."

Hardly had Holmes spoken when both men became aware of loud, animated talking at the front entrance. The footman's protestations were audible, as well as a much louder, and very angry, voice. Then, the frightened servant appeared in the drawing room just ahead of two others, one of them a tall, husky fellow whom Wilde recognized as Sean McConnell, a member of the police force. Wilde rose from his chair to introduce Holmes to the Marquess of Queensberry, though Holmes recognised him at once. However, before any such courtesies could be observed, the intruder spoke, or rather shouted, first.

"Sit down!"

Wilde drew calmly on his cigarette and then said slowly: "I do not allow anyone to talk like that to me in my house or anywhere else." He turned to Holmes: "Mr. Holmes, I must apologise for this very unexpected interruption." Holmes made a gesture to indicate that his host should not trouble himself about it. Turning back to Queensberry, Wilde continued in a calm voice: "I suppose you have come to apologise for the statement you made about my wife and myself in letters you wrote to your son."

"I've come for no such reason," said the slightly calmer Queensberry, who was clearly taken aback by Wilde's serene manner.

"I should have the right any day," said Wilde, "to prosecute you for writing such a letter."

"It was privileged, as it was written to my son."

"But how dare you say such things about your son and me?" demanded Wilde with fervour.

Queensberry pondered his next statement, then exclaimed, "You *were* kicked out of the Savoy Hotel at a moment's notice for your disgusting conduct!"

"That is a lie!"

"And you've taken furnished rooms for him in Piccadilly." He took a sheet of paper from his pocket, held it up, and tapped it with his finger. "Here's the address."

"Somebody has been telling you an absurd set of lies about your son and me. I've done nothing of the kind."

The excited nobleman persisted in his charges, and Wilde broke in with an implied warning: "Lord Queensberry, do you seriously accuse your son and me of improper conduct?"

The unwelcome visitor stopped, looked uneasily at Holmes, and said cautiously: "I don't say you *are* it, but you *look* it and you *pose* it, which is just as bad." With renewed vehemence he exclaimed, "If I catch you and my son together again in any public place, I will thrash you!"

Wilde slowly placed his cigarette into an ashtray. "Sir, I don't know what the Queensberry rules of boxing are, but the Oscar Wilde rule is to shoot at sight." Wilde pointed toward the door. "Now, leave my house at once!"

The marquess and his companion turned to leave, but Queensberry stopped and looked back. "It's a disgusting scandal!"

"If it is so, you are the author of the scandal and no one else."

Queensberry sneered and exclaimed, "Let's get out of here, McConnell! We shall have to bathe with disinfectant!"

Wilde's young footman had been nervously observing everything from a safe place near the room's entrance. Wilde got his attention and said, "This is the Marquess of Queensberry, the most infamous brute in London. You are never to allow him to enter my house again!" Wilde quickly left the drawing room, went to the front door, opened it, and said sternly to the marquess and McConnell, "Now! Get out!"

After the visitors had left, Wilde and Holmes sat and discussed what had happened.

"This is quite the climax of everything!" exclaimed Wilde. "I see no alternative except a legal prosecution. Lord Alfred Douglas has been begging me to take the lunatic to court. He says that his family will pay the legal expenses. I believe I must do so."

Holmes shook his head. "That, I think, you must *not* do. Of course, I am not a lawyer; and before you do anything else in this matter, I strongly urge you to speak with someone familiar with the law—a solicitor, for instance. But, of course, this really is no concern of mine."

"Oh, I'm very interested in what you think! Besides, your excellent handling of the photographic mystery certainly gives you a right to express an opinion in this wearisome matter."

"Well, then, I think you must avoid any sort of legal confrontation with Queensberry. I believe further that he is, in fact, trying to goad you into doing just that. But you'd have nothing to gain and much to lose. It's obvious that the man is mentally unbalanced and, therefore, very dangerous. Also, you'd have the disadvantage of seeming to be coming between a son and his father."

"But Lord Alfred is an adult, and this man is only a grotesque caricature of a father!"

"That's certainly true," conceded Holmes, "but a jury of everyday London citizens might not understand that."

"Wilde rose from his chair, walked to the window, and looked out. "Thank Heaven," he said softly, "that Constance and the children were not here!" He turned to Holmes and said flatly, "I fear I myself am not an *ideal husband*, Mr. Holmes."

"Perhaps," said Holmes dryly, "the only way to avoid being judged one way or the other is to remain a bachelor."

"You have never met anyone you wished to marry?"

Holmes shook his head. "Never. I live too unconventional a life. No woman would tolerate it—and I could not tolerate *that*. Oh, I once encountered a young woman whom I still remember as one of the most remarkable persons I've ever known." He paused while his face took on a faraway look. "As my friend Dr. Watson has said, to me she is always *The Woman*!"

"Was she a client?"

"No, an adversary. But a most worthy adversary—and person. She was charming, beautiful, and intelligent." He smiled wryly. "She revealed my client as the scoundrel *he* was!"

"Ah," exclaimed Wilde, "she sounds most formidable—and familiar! I seem to recall someone like that in Dr. Watson's 'A Scandal in Bohemia.' Irene Adler—wasn't that her name?"

"No, that's the name that Watson used to protect her privacy. I'm flattered, Mr. Wilde, that you've taken an interest in my work."

"Oh, indeed I have," said Wilde. "In fact, it has occurred to me that Irene Adler's story would be an excellent subject for dramatic treatment." He returned to his chair and sat down slowly. Since he clearly was preparing to say something, Holmes remained silent.

"Mr. Holmes, I am most grateful for the help you've already given me. But I'd be even more grateful if you would consent to advise me in my more pressing problem with Queensberry."

Holmes shook his head vigorously. "No, you don't want my help. You need one of the best barristers that London affords, and I could suggest several."

Wilde nodded. "I fully agree with you, but I'm speaking of advice other than legal."

"I shall always be available for consultation with you about any matter that falls within my area of professional competence." Holmes rose to leave but paused to say, "I regard you as one of the greatest writers in the English-speaking world today, and I hope that nothing will interfere with your continued enrichment of our language."

Wilde was greatly moved but managed to say: "Thank you, Mr. Holmes, and goodbye. I look forward to our meeting again."

"As do I, Mr. Wilde. Goodbye."

The footman showed Holmes out, and Wilde resumed his seat. He took a cigarette, lit it, and drew upon it as though it held the solution to all his problems.

The confrontation with Queensberry had shaken Wilde badly, but his recent lack of sleep overcame his disquiet. When his young servant entered the drawing room, he found his employer asleep and called softly to him. Wilde stirred, opened his eyes, sat up, and ran his fingers through his hair.

"Mr. Wilde, you have a visitor."

Wilde smiled groggily and said, "Indeed? Who is it?"

"Lord Alfred Douglas."

Wilde paused, looked first at his servant, and then gazed about the room as though unsure what to do next. With an air of resignation he asked where Douglas was.

"In your study, sir."

"Have my family returned yet?"

"No, sir."

"Very well. Please show him in here." Wilde quickly added, "No, wait—I'll join him there."

Wilde entered his study just as Douglas was helping himself to a bottle of brandy.

"Will you join me, Oscar?"

"I think not; perhaps later." Wilde settled into a chair and turned toward his visitor. "Bosie, your father was here about an hour ago."

Douglas frowned. "What did he come here for?"

"Why does he ever go anywhere except to make someone's life wretched?" Wilde shook his head slowly. "He was insulting—appallingly insulting. He made horrible charges." Strong emotion forced Wilde to cease talking.

"Were you alone?"

"My family, thank God, had already left and are still out. But I did have a visitor."

"Who?"

After a moment of hesitation, Wilde somewhat reluctantly told Douglas that Sherlock Holmes had visited. The younger man was greatly surprised to hear this. "He's some sort of detective, isn't he? What does he have to do with you?"

"Mr. Holmes has been very helpful to me recently. I had been getting some insolent, harassing postings that I assumed came from your father."

"And did they?"

"Holmes has demonstrated rather conclusively that they did not, that in fact they came instead from Jimmy Whistler." Wilde then explained the nature of the photographs and how the detective reached his conclusions. "Mr. Holmes is one of the most brilliant persons I've ever met. He is practical in areas that are totally foreign to my own nature. And he has been very comforting."

"Oscar, I'm hurt that I'm now hearing this for the first time." Douglas looked petulantly away from Wilde, then faced him again. "I thought we had a special relationship."

"We do, Bosie, we do. Of course we do, but I feared that you were too closely associated with all that has happened to be objective."

"Well, I appreciate *that*!"

"Now, you must not take that personally."

"How else *should* I take it?" exclaimed Douglas. "I'm told that I'm not objective and that my closest friend cannot trust me enough to confide in me!"

"Now, Bosie, this isn't fair. You, of all people, know what a bitter relationship you have with your father—in fact, how both you and your brothers regard your father. I needed someone who was absolutely disinterested and—well, someone who could give me practical advice—advice free of emotion."

Douglas had turned away in anger. He faced Wilde again and exploded. "And just what great wisdom did this fellow Holmes come up with?"

"Now, Bosie, you're being bitter!"

"What the devil *should* I be?" Douglas looked away and, without turning back to Wilde, said slowly: "I asked you what *ineffable* advice the great detective *vouchsafed* to you?"

"Bosie, I don't think this is a good time to go into the matter."

"I think it's a damned admirable time! I'll bet you can hardly wait to explain it to Robbie Ross!"

Though Wilde was by nature slow to anger, he was now beginning to resent Douglas's sarcasm. "I'll tell Robbie soon enough."

"*Oh, I'm sure you will!*" shrieked Douglas. "But tell him *what?*"

"That Holmes thinks I would be insane to bring libel charges against Lord Queensberry, as you want me to do."

Douglas looked incredulously at Wilde. Then, without another word, he jumped up and stamped out. As he exited the front door, he slammed it.

Bosie's bitter words and stormy exit, coming on top of Queensberry's visit, left Wilde temporarily in shock. He spied the bottle of brandy that Bosie had opened; and after pouring himself a generous portion, he sat in his chair and greedily emptied the glass, then started more slowly on a second one. After a quiet interval, he rose slowly and moved unsteadily about the room. His footman came to the study's entrance and asked whether he could do anything for his master. Wilde glanced at his watch. "No. I shall go out and probably won't return until sometime in the evening."

Wilde stepped outside and hired a hansom. After telling the driver to go to an address near Cavendish Square, he settled back into his seat and tried to lose himself in the passing scenes of a city that he loved, or at least a city that he *had* loved. Was it now to become hateful? In his distressed solitude he imagined himself pursued by Nemesis. *Have I offended the gods? Am*

I guilty of hubris? He saw his exquisite life in ominous disarray and danger, and in his troubled reverie composed a bit of verse:

The tower of ivory is assailed by loathsome things,
And on the thirsty sand is now my life-blood spilt...

The cab's arrival at his palmist's address interrupted his meditations. He dismounted and paid his fare. Already he was feeling less tense when he stepped to the door and sounded the knocker. The door opened and there was Madame Marisepehr in all her exotic beauty.

"Ah, Mr. Wilde! How good to see you again. Won't you come in?" She escorted him to his favourite chair in her parlour. "And now, Mr. Wilde, may I bring you something to drink—a cup of tea, or perhaps a glass of wine? I have just opened a bottle of very good Chablis." She stopped, then exclaimed: "But wait, I have a better idea! Let me get you a glass of a very special wine that we enjoy in Persia."

"You are very kind, Madame. But before leaving home I had some brandy. Perhaps it's better that I just talk with you."

"Of course, Mr. Wilde." She moved an ottoman closer to him and, sitting upon it, asked, "And what exactly would you like to talk about?" With that question, she reached out and took his hand. After studying it and running her fingers over areas of his palm, she looked at him through beautiful but concerned eyes.

"Mr. Wilde, I think you are greatly troubled about something."

"Yes, dear Sybil. I live for poetry, but am obliged to do so in a crassly prosaic world. I sometimes fear I've gone insane and wonder how I got there." With a bitter chuckle Wilde murmured: "How I got there, indeed! All roads lead there, and London has become a madhouse!"

"Mr. Wilde, you certainly are *not* insane!"

He nodded slowly. "Alas, dear Sybil, you are correct; for were I insane, I would be deliciously happy." Wilde sat up, took out his wallet, and extracted ten pounds, which he handed to Marisepehr. "Please, take this, my good friend. And now let me hear charming things from one who, in exchange, takes mere pieces of paper!"

Marisepehr rose and poured Wilde a glass of wine. "But first I want you to enjoy this excellent wine from my country."

Wilde brightened noticeably and took the proffered glass. "You are most kind, Madame." He sipped it and exclaimed: "It is indeed excellent! How does Persia manage to produce so outstanding a wine?"

"Probably, Mr. Wilde, because it is forbidden by our religion."

"Yes, that *is* always a great inspiration to any art."

"And now, Mr. Wilde, give me your hand."

He did so and she proceeded to stroke it gently, from time to time murmuring obscure, sonorous things. Wilde leaned back, relaxed, and closed his eyes. His face revealed a pleased weariness. Marisepehr then looked closely at his palm, traced with her index finger certain areas and lines, and clucked softly. Every so often she hummed Persian tunes and occasionally murmured in Farsi. Suddenly she exclaimed, "Aha!"

Wilde opened his eyes and looked questioningly at her. "My dear Sybil, what do you find?"

She looked at him keenly and said with emphasis, "I see much success for you; you will be at even greater heights!" She looked more closely and was silent for a moment.

"Is that all?" Wilde asked.

"I'm—uncertain," she said hesitantly. Moving her finger across his palm, she added, "I see—I see your career advance steadily and successfully, and then..."

Wilde waited for her to finish her thought. When she did not, he somewhat uneasily said, "Yes, and then what?"

"Well, I'm unsure how to interpret what I see here." She tapped an index finger lightly on one area of his palm. "You are the most famous man in England—one of the most famous in Europe. That is clear. But I suddenly come to—something— something *else*. I'm not sure what to call it; it's almost like— well, I'm uncertain what." She veered in a new direction. "Now, here I see you in some sort of public event."

"In a theatre?

She paused then shook her head slowly. "Perhaps, but it seems to be something more official."

Wilde sat up. "Dear Sybil, could it be a courtroom?"

"A courtroom? That's *possible*. Yes! I believe it *is* a court-room, for I see robed men in funny wigs." She began to speak more rapidly and with less uncertainty. "I hear your name be-ing mentioned, Mr. Wilde."

"Am I the plaintiff?"

She looked up at Wilde inquiringly. "Plaintiff? I do not know this word."

"The aggrieved party in a case at law. Have you been in a British courtroom, Sybil?"

"Yes, once."

"And where do you see me sitting?"

"Let's see." Suddenly Marisepehr exclaimed, "I see you now; you are not sitting; you are standing and speaking."

"You mean I'm giving evidence?"

"Yes, I think that's it."

Wilde is clearly excited by this information, and he asks very slowly, "Can you tell me how this will turn out?"

Madame Marisepehr looked at Wilde, then at his palm. She seemed to be struggling with something. With a troubled expression on her face she turned to her client, then turned away from him and said in a low, dispirited voice, "I see you entirely successful in whatever it is you are trying to do."

"My dear Sybil, this is wonderful news! This calls for another glass of that excellent Persian wine, for I must drink a toast to you and your wonderful powers."

After the two of them finished their glasses, Wilde rose. "Madame, I really must go. I have so much to do, and you have shown me the direction I must take to do it."

The seeress nodded sadly. "Of course, Mr. Wilde." She rose when Wilde did and her eyes followed him closely as he moved toward the door. Then, suddenly she ran toward him and exclaimed: "No! No! You must *not* do it."

Wilde stopped, turned, and looked inquiringly at her. "Dear Sybil! I don't understand. What must I not do?"

"Whatever it is you are planning. I did not tell you everything I saw. There is danger gathering around you! Everything is wrong with the images I beheld. The *colours!* The colours were *all wrong.* The figures I saw were wrong—the expression on the face of the judge was horrible. Nothing was right!" She stopped to control her emotions, then continued. "And worst of all"—she shook her head rapidly and almost whispered—"worst of all I saw—a *wall!*"

Wilde was perplexed. "A wall! What sort of wall, dear Sybil?"

"I don't know. But it was a wall of huge, gray stones, and you were standing beside it. You appeared very sad and alone."

She looked almost pleadingly at Wilde. "And I saw you enter a gate through that wall!"

Wilde took her hands, patted them, and held them. "You must not be troubled by that vision. That was how I was before I arrived here today. The city was closing in upon me, and I felt trapped with nowhere to turn. But your company and your delightful hospitality, and especially your great insight, have dispelled all that." With a smile he gently raised her hands to his lips and kissed them. "I don't think you understand how talented and charming you are. Goodbye, dear Sybil."

Marisepehr saw Wilde out and then, very depressed, sank slowly into a chair.

Chapter 4

Wilde, now immeasurably relieved by his visit to Madame Marisepehr, suddenly had the desire to talk again with Holmes. He directed his driver to go by the Baker Street address. As the hansom pulled up to 221-B, Holmes and Watson had just stepped outside their residence. Watson recognized Wilde and called to him.

"We were just going to the Café Royal for a late lunch. Would you honour us with your company?"

Wilde accepted their invitation gladly, for he had eaten little that day. He paid his cab driver while Holmes hailed a four-wheeler that would offer them ample room and a chance to chat. On the way to the restaurant Holmes explained to Wilde that he had informed Watson about Queensberry's disturbing visit earlier that day.

"I hope you understand, Mr. Wilde, that Watson is my professional associate. I have always found his discretion and sound commonsense of inestimable value. You have entrusted me with your information, and I assure you that Watson is as deserving of your confidence."

"Oh, I'm sure he is, and I'm very content to have his thoughts and confidence in this wearisome business. Moreover, it will be a pleasure to share a table again with you both." Wilde went on to tell them about his recent unpleasant scene with Alfred Douglas and the latter's annoyance at learning of Holmes' advice against prosecuting Queensberry.

"Was this outburst typical?" asked Holmes.

"I fear so. He is furious that I had not yet discussed this with him."

"Why?" asked Watson. "Does he think you're obliged to do that?"

After a pause Wilde said: "Dr. Watson, Bosie, despite his terrible relations with his father, seems to have many of Queensberry's characteristics. He is dogmatic and demanding. As much as I like Bosie, I must say that he always thinks his word is law for everyone—except himself, of course."

"Well," said Holmes, "I advise you to resist any urge to cater to Lord Alfred's wishes in this matter."

"Yes, indeed," said Watson. "I fully agree with Holmes on this. Everything I've heard about Queensberry makes me say that it would be very unwise to try to prosecute him. Anyone, except perhaps Her Majesty's government, must come out no better than second-best."

At this point the four-wheeler stopped in front of the Café Royal. The three men left their carriage and entered the restaurant. There they were greeted by the *maître d'hôtel*, who looked about the restaurant and exclaimed, "Ah, gentlemen, I have just the place for you, where you can enjoy conversation without being disturbed." The three men followed him to the table; but before they could take their places, a man walked over to them.

"Hello, Oscar, what a pleasure to see you. It's been quite a while."

Wilde looked up and saw Frank Harris. "Frank, how good to see you. Where are you sitting?"

Harris pointed to another table a short distance away and said, "Well, I'm sitting just over there. In fact, I'm expecting Bernard Shaw at any moment."

Holmes observed that their table was quite large and could easily accommodate both Harris and Shaw. "So, you really must join us, sir." Harris accepted the invitation and informed his waiter.

Wilde turned to his two companions. "Mr. Sherlock Holmes and Dr. John Watson, may I introduce Mr. Frank Harris, London's finest editor?" The three men shook hands. "Frank has been editor of some of London's foremost periodicals. In fact, Frank, I'm shocked to see you in the Café Royal. I thought you dined only on manuscripts."

"Not anymore. I find most of them quite underdone and indigestible." Turning to Wilde's companions, he said: "Mr. Holmes, I've heard and read quite a lot about your most unusual work and have long wished to meet you." To Watson he said: "And, Dr. Watson, I'm a great admirer of your accounts of Mr. Holmes's exploits. But I'm very jealous of the *Strand Magazine's* good fortune in having you as a contributor."

"You are most kind, Mr. Harris."

"And you are most talented, Dr. Watson. I believe you practice medicine, too, do you not?"

"I do, sir, when I'm not otherwise employed with Holmes's investigations."

Turning to Wilde, Harris asked whether he had had any more trouble with Queensberry."

"That, Frank, is the experience of everyone who knows the howling marquess." Gesturing toward Holmes, Wilde said, "And just this morning Mr. Holmes had the misfortune to meet the wretched scion of the Douglas clan. Queensberry favored me with an unexpected visit."

"Oh," said Holmes, "it was nothing greatly outside my experience. Indeed, aberrations of character provide my livelihood, just as physical ones serve Dr. Watson."

Harris looked across the dining area and exclaimed, "Ah, there's Shaw." Even as Harris spoke, Shaw saw them and approached their table. With a chuckle he said, "Wilde, I just saw your old friend Jimmy Whistler outside." He chortled. "I think he misses you very much. Shall I ask him in?"

"My dear Shaw," said Wilde, "I think not. But, you've just solved my problem of a proper sacrifice for Lent. Giving up Jimmy should put me on the threshold of sainthood! By the way, Mr. Holmes, I believe Jimmy Whistler has dropped his efforts to achieve in paint what I did much more effectively in prose." Wilde then told Harris and Shaw about Whistler's recent mailings of the evolving portrait. "I've received no more of his wretched demonstrations of life clumsily imitating art."

Since Shaw continued to stand while talking with the other four, Wilde exclaimed, "You really must join us, Shaw. After all, Frank is reckless enough to do so, and you spend your time defying British conventions and assumptions." Shaw readily accepted the invitation, and Wilde introduced him to Holmes and Watson.

"Mr. Shaw," said Watson, "I always enjoy your writing, and I congratulate you on your recent play, *Arms and the Man*."

"Thank you, Dr. Watson. You know, this is quite a coincidence; for I had been told that there was indeed someone in London, other than myself, who liked it. I'm delighted to learn his identity."

"Very amusing, Shaw!" exclaimed Harris. "But you must surely realise that ridiculing war is a dangerous pastime in British society."

"It is, indeed," said Wilde. "You also have gone to a lot of trouble when all you needed to do was to show merely that war is vulgar. When you are able to do that, the British public will cease admiring it. But you must also be careful to avoid the criticism that I've been receiving."

"And what's that?" asked Shaw.

"That I'm conceited."

"Oh, *that*!" exclaimed Shaw with a snort. "Well, I make no apology for *my* conceit. After all, the important point is not that one is conceited but whether one has anything to be conceited about."

"Yes," said Wilde, "modesty *is* simply the conceit of the timid, is it not? Besides, Shaw, we're both Irishmen, and our task is to educate the English; and all devices suitable to that end are in order. Imagine how greatly civilisation would be benefitted if the Irish could learn how to listen and the English how to talk."

"Exactly," exclaimed Shaw. "And that's what I'm working on. I'm bursting with good ideas to disturb their ignorance. I need only to put them before the British public."

"Isn't this a little presumptuous, Shaw?" asked Harris.

"Oh, it is, indeed—*more* than a little. I confess to being presumptuous and dare you to try to refute it! All the great men of history have been. Look at Columbus, for instance. He presumed there was land to the west and found it."

"Yes," drawled Wilde, "but not a very nice land."

"Anyway," said Harris, "how would you go about this great, *presumptuous* project of intruding upon British ignorance?"

"Oh, there are any number of ways, Frank. My first method will be to start a periodical that will present my ideas to the reading public."

"Interesting," murmured Wilde. "But you must start with a very imaginative and arresting name for your magazine. Have you thought of one?"

"Of course," exclaimed Shaw, "since my purpose would be to impress the public with my own personality and ideas, I'd naturally call it *Shaw's Magazine*: You know, *Shaw—Shaw— Shaw*!" and he banged his fist on the table at each syllable.

"I see," said Wilde, "and how would you spell that?"

Shaw laughed as loudly as did the others.

After the frivolity, Wilde's face assumed a serious cast. "Shaw, it must be providential that you're here."

"It hadn't occurred to me that Providence even knew I existed. But assuming it does, may I ask why you slander Providence with such a reckless charge?"

Wilde turned to Harris and said, "Frank, Shaw's question gets us back to my trouble with Queensberry..."

Harris broke in before Wilde could finish his statement: "Oscar, I'm familiar with this matter but are you trying to insure that everyone else in London knows it, too?"

"I've informed Mr. Holmes and Dr. Watson, Frank, and am quite willing that Shaw be informed."

Shaw shifted his position in his chair and cleared his throat. "Wilde, I know already a little about it but had the impression that this matter had improved."

"Hardly. If anything, it has entered a new stage, and that an intolerable one."

Holmes and Watson looked startled. "But Mr. Wilde," said Holmes, "my hope was that you had decided to ignore his antics."

"Yes, indeed!" exclaimed Watson.

Wilde spread his hands in a gesture of futility. "The matter is now up to him. If he ceases his provocations and keeps his distance, I shall be satisfied to do nothing. But unfortunately, I know him too well to expect that."

Holmes leaned forward. "But you and I discussed the problems that a prosecution would entail. How would you proceed?"

"I assume that Queensberry will try to use my writings against me, and I feel certain that I can deal successfully with him if he does." He turned to Harris. "Frank, would you be willing, if it comes to a trial, to testify as to the literary quality of my works?"

"Of course. But are you sure that would be the only issue?"

"With Queensberry, who can be *sure* of anything?" asked Wilde with a shake of his head. "He makes the dogma of an actual Hell almost credible."

"You must always keep in mind," cautioned Holmes, "his efforts to get some of your correspondence. He's evidently delving much more deeply into your life than just your literary pieces."

"There's nothing in my letters that would help him in any way."

Shaw looked keenly at Wilde. "Are you certain of that?"

"Completely."

Obviously unsatisfied, Shaw added, "Well, if you think my testimony about your writings would be of any use in a legal contest, I should be entirely willing to give it."

"Thank you very much, Shaw. I was intending to ask you for your help." Looking at both Shaw and Harris he said, "The comments of both you gentlemen, with regard to my writings, would be most helpful and carry great weight."

"Well, I'm sure that Frank's testimony would be respectfully received," said Shaw. "But don't forget that I'm 'Shaw, the buffoon'—'Shaw, the clown.'"

During all this exchange, Holmes' face registered puzzlement. At a lull in the conversation he asked Wilde what had changed his mind since their earlier discussion of this matter.

"I have come to the conclusion that I have on my side the much better case. I've also recently had some encouraging information as to my chances in a legal confrontation with Queensberry."

"What sort of encouraging information?" asked Holmes. "I hope it was from a competent legal authority."

"That, Mr. Holmes, I'm not yet at liberty to discuss."

At this point Lord Alfred Douglas walked over to the table. The other men had not seen him approach, but Bosie immediately exchanged greetings with them. Harris's booming voice invited the young man to join them. At first Douglas hesitated and merely looked glumly at Wilde.

"Of course, Bosie, we'd be delighted if you would," said Wilde. Douglas took a chair from nearby and sat down, though nearer Harris and Shaw than toWilde.

Making a point of looking right at Douglas, Wilde said: "Bosie, I hadn't realized you were here. I think you'll be pleased to learn that I've completely reexamined what we were discussing. I feel certain that you are right and that a prosecution of your father would certainly be a good strategy if he insists on provoking one."

"Oscar!" exclaimed Douglas, "I'm delighted!   What changed your mind?"

"Oh, it's a rather complicated matter, and I'll explain later. Both Harris and Shaw have consented to vouch for the literary value of my writings. That will be invaluable." Turning to Harris and Shaw he said, "And, gentlemen, I hope it goes without saying that you have my undying gratitude."

But most of those around the table were clearly disturbed by what Wilde had just said, Holmes perhaps more than the others. He said quietly, "Mr. Wilde, in light of our earlier discussion of this, I can't understand how your ideas have been so altered."

"I think this would be very unwise, too, Oscar," said Harris as he tugged at his moustache. Watson and Shaw seconded what Harris and Holmes had said.

Lord Alfred jumped up and exclaimed: "This is outrageous! You men are certainly not Oscar's friends!" He turned to Wilde and shouted, "I hope you have more backbone than to listen to them!"

Wilde was visibly displeased with the young man's outburst. Glancing around the table he softly said: "All these gentlemen have only my best interests in mind. They haven't fully examined all the issues involved. I shall explain everything to them in good time. In the meantime, Bosie, we must not insult our friends."

Harris looked at Wilde and then at Douglas. "I still think that you would be making a very serious mistake to pursue this idea."

"That's because you don't know what you're talking about!" shouted Douglas. "Friends! You aren't Oscar's friends—*none* of you!" He quickly rose, looked around the table, and then said to Wilde, "Don't pay any attention to what they're saying, Oscar." For good measure he repeated his first charge that they were not acting as friends should. He then turned abruptly and left.

Wilde was clearly upset and, for once, speechless. Finally, he rose and started to follow Douglas. He stopped, turned around, and said to Harris, "That really is *not* very friendly of you, Frank." And with that he followed Douglas out.

After Douglas and Wilde had left, Shaw said, "Oscar's completely besotted with Bosie Douglas!"

"So is Bosie Douglas!" grumbled Harris. "Mr. Holmes, what do you and Dr. Watson make of all this?"

Holmes shook his head. "Nothing positive—nothing good at all! Mr. Wilde asked me recently my opinion of his instituting charges against Queensberry. I strongly advised against it, and I had thought he agreed with me."

"What do you suppose has happened since then, Holmes?" asked Watson.

"Bosie Douglas must have somehow managed to change his mind," said Shaw.

Holmes looked at Shaw, then at Harris. With a slight shrug he said, "I don't think so. Otherwise, why was Douglas so surprised by Wilde's change of heart? I think there's some other element here." He turned to his associate. "Watson, do you recall our conversation with Wilde during our drive here?"

"Much of it. Why?"

"He said something about having just come from a good friend's home. He didn't give a name, but I recall hearing him at least once refer to this person as *she*." Holmes asked Harris and Shaw whether either of them knew of any woman that Wilde might be visiting.

Harris, after a moment of silence, said that he had heard Wilde speak once or twice about a woman whose opinions he was inclined to value rather highly. "Some sort of fortune teller, I think," he added with a disdainful grimace.

The other three men traded incredulous glances, and Shaw chortled. "Fortune teller! And this from a fellow who threatens to found a men's order called 'The Confraternity of the Faithless'!" This elicited smiles from the others.

Holmes broke in suddenly. "Watson, do you remember the driver of Mr. Wilde's cab when he stopped earlier today in Baker Street?"

"Yes, but I don't know his name."

"Well, I think I do," said Holmes as he rose from the table. "Gentlemen, it has been a great pleasure to meet you. I hope you'll excuse me as I try to find some clue as to what forces are governing Mr. Wilde's strange actions. I'll let you know if I can do so." He turned to Watson and suggested that he remain with their guests.

"Very well, Holmes. I'll see you later today. I wish you success. Let me know if I can help in any way."

Holmes had little trouble finding the driver who had picked up Wilde and taken him to Baker Street. This man was immediately able to tell at which address Wilde had hired him. Moreover, the cab driver told Holmes about the beautiful Persian palmist and added the extra information that Wilde was one of her best customers. Holmes asked to be taken to that address. A few minutes later Holmes alighted from his hansom, paid the driver well, and stepped over to the substantial entrance. Only one use of the knocker was necessary. At once Holmes beheld a striking-looking woman who was perhaps about forty years old.

Tipping his hat, Holmes introduced himself and asked, "Am I addressing Madame Marisepehr?"

She acknowledged that he was, and expressed surprise that he pronounced her name correctly.

"Ah, on my way from Tibet to Mecca, three years ago, I spent some time in Persia and learned something of your language."

"How interesting, Mr. Holmes! Is this a professional call?"

"In a way, Madame, but on behalf of another person."

"Sir, may I ask whom?"

"Mr. Oscar Wilde. I'm a private consulting detective, Madame, and Mr. Wilde has recently been a client."

She nodded and looked sombre. "Won't you come in, sir?" She showed Holmes to a chair and seated herself on a sofa. "And now, Mr. Holmes, how may I help you?"

"Madame Marisepehr, in order to save time I shall assume that Mr. Wilde has consulted you about the Marquess of Queensberry. Is this correct?"

The palmist was silent but clearly disturbed by the question. Holmes, in some frustration, exclaimed, "Please, Madame, we probably do not have much time, and I am trying to keep Mr. Wilde from making a great miscalculation. I must beg you not to be coy with me, and I shall be frank with you." Her continued silence and obvious discomfort led Holmes to assure her that he intended no harm to Wilde.

She shook her head sadly. "That's what *he* said, too."

"Who, Madame?"

"Lord Queensberry.   He came here once to ask about Mr. Wilde."

"In regard to what, Madame Marisepehr?"

Still struggling with this discussion, she closed her eyes and shook her head in frustration. "Mr. Holmes, I don't like to discuss my clients, but I'm so disturbed by all this that I think I must."

"I agree, Madame, for neither of us wishes Mr. Wilde to act foolishly."

She then explained to Holmes all that had happened, of how Queensberry had paid her to advise Wilde to prosecute him, and how she had agreed to do so.

"And did you so advise Mr. Wilde?" asked Holmes.

"I'm ashamed to say that I did tell Mr. Wilde that he would succeed in his legal action. But I was then conscience stricken, and before he left I strongly begged him not to. I warned him strongly that I sensed danger in what he was planning. It was useless, however, for he was so excited by my first prediction that he completely discounted my warning." She clasped her hands and looked earnestly at her visitor. "Mr. Holmes, I am very fond of Mr. Wilde and would be greatly distressed if he met some calamity."

"Indeed, Madame Marisepehr, as would I and many others." Holmes lifted a warning finger. "And I should say that Lord Queensberry is a dangerous, desperate man. I strongly urge you to have nothing more to do with him."

Marisepehr nodded quickly several times and brushed away tears with her handkerchief. "I shall certainly take your advice."

Holmes rose. "Madame, I thank you for your helpful information. And now there is much to do to try to save our friend from destroying himself."

Rising, the palmist held out her hand, which Holmes took in both of his, saying as he did so: "And please, dear Madame Marisepehr, be very careful for your own safety in the immediate future. We cannot discount the possibility that Queensberry will try to harm you."

"I shall certainly be careful, Mr. Holmes."

"Neither Dr. Watson, my associate, nor I will give any hint of your assistance. Nevertheless, are you able to identify your callers before you open your door?"

"Yes, Mr. Holmes, through these front windows."

"Then, be sure to do so."

"Have no fear, dear Mr. Holmes, I shall. And may your efforts be successful. I hope you will apprise me of any further help that I may be able to give."

"I shall indeed, my dear lady. Goodbye."

After she had closed her door, Marisepehr, through tearful eyes, looked out her window at the departing Holmes.

Chapter 5

Watson was out seeing a patient; and Holmes, at work on his writing, heard his landlady answer the door. He looked at his watch—eight-thirty. Who would be calling so early on so cold a morning? The unmistakable voice of Scotland Yard's Inspector Lestrade, in the outside hall, answered his question. A knock at the door elicited Holmes's "Come in!" Mrs. Hudson appeared with the inspector immediately behind her.

"Thank you, Mrs. Hudson! Ah, Lestrade," exclaimed Holmes, "come in! Do sit over there and I'll join you at once." Holmes set aside his work and immediately seated himself near Lestrade. "And now, what could have persuaded Scotland Yard to send their most illustrious detective out so early—and in this extremely cold weather—to visit me in Baker Street?"

"Well, Mr. Holmes, crime does not defer to snow and ice, and neither can I."

"Of course. I pity the poor criminal who mistakenly assumes you do. But surely there's nothing afoot in London that you and The Yard can't handle."

Lestrade smiled complacently. "No, nothing out of the ordinary. But there was a murder last night; and as soon as I surveyed the scene, I realised it presents some aspects that might interest you. And, after all, though your methods are somewhat unorthodox, you *have* been helpful to us once or twice in the past."

"My dear fellow, you flatter me. But I am always delighted to throw whatever light I can on a case." Holmes rose and went to a table where there was a coffee pot over a spirit flame. "Would you have some coffee to help recover from the cold morning?"

"Yes, indeed, thank you!"

Holmes poured two cups, kept one and handed the other to Lestrade. He seated himself and addressed his visitor, "Now, sir, tell me the particulars."

Lestrade took a prodigious gulp of his coffee. "Well, the victim is one of our policemen, Sean McConnell. His body was discovered early this morning by several young children playing in the snow. He was not on duty and was not wearing his uniform." To Holmes's question about suspects, the inspector replied that though they did not yet have any, there were some clues that seemed promising. After relating a few more details, Lestrade emptied his cup and looked over at the coffeepot. "If you don't mind, I think I'd fancy a bit more coffee. I must have been much colder than I'd realised."

"Of course." Holmes took the pot over and refilled his visitor's cup. "And now, Lestrade, where did this happen?"

"Let me have three or four more swallows of this excellent coffee, and I'll take you to the place."

On the way to the scene Lestrade explained what was known about the crime. McConnell's body had been found on the edge of St. James's Park in a place where there was a thick growth of evergreen shrubbery. An investigation had so far found no weapon, though the officer had been stabbed with a knife or something similar. It was a throat wound, and the detective assumed that McConnell had strangled on his own blood. Even if he had called for help, there probably had been few persons in the area to hear him that late and on so cold a night.

Their cab reached the crime site and the two men got out of their carriage. Lestrade pointed and said, "Right over this way, Mr. Holmes, where you see all the trampled snow."

After going about halfway to the place, Holmes stopped, observed the scene, and shook his head in irritation. "How many clues must now be effaced!"

"Well," exclaimed Lestrade, "we haven't been exactly sleeping. I put our man Culbertson on the job at once."

Keenly surveying the area, Holmes nodded and said, "He's one of your better investigators."

"Yes," said Lestrade, "and by that time he had some early daylight in which to work, though the snow has made his task difficult."

The two men stepped carefully in the direction of the spot where the body had been found, with Holmes constantly observing the various impressions in the snow. Closer to the site more tracks were visible. Holmes bent down to examine them, then glanced up at the falling snow that seemed about to cease. He stood again and searched the entire area between him and

the street, concentrating particularly on the various sets of footprints. Then, some distance from where the body had lain,
something caught his attention and he walked toward it.

"Mr. Holmes," exclaimed Lestrade, "the body was over *here*."

"Yes, Lestrade, but let me check something else first."
He walked over to the edge of the lawn, near the street, and
crouched down to examine two sets of footprints in parallel
tracks. Pointing to them, he said, half to himself, "Two persons
walked along here."

Lestrade, who had moved over to where Holmes was, said,
"Well, Mr. Holmes, *many* have been walking here!"

Holmes looked up quickly. "Yes, of course. Well, now let's take
a look at where you found the body." Lestrade glanced at an officer
standing guard nearby and made a little grimace of impatience.

The area where the body had fallen was much disturbed,
not only by the feet of the investigators but also by what had
obviously been a struggle. There was a considerable deposit
of blood on the snow where the dead policeman's body had
fallen and had lain, apparently for several hours. The shrubbery, sheathed in ice, had been damaged as well by the officer's
struggle with his attacker. Even much ice on the protective
wrought-iron railing around the plants had been shattered. A
much smaller quantity of blood several feet away from where
the victim had lain caught the detective's attention.

"Interesting," murmured Holmes.

Lestrade looked up quickly. "Have we missed something,
Mr. Holmes?"

"Perhaps not. Who can say at this point?"

Seeing Holmes's interest in the second deposit of blood,
Lestrade said, "Our officer apparently had already fallen once
before he collapsed finally."

"Very possibly. Where is McConnell's body?"

"At the morgue"

"May we go there?"

"Of course," said Lestrade. "Have you seen all here that you wish?"

Holmes glanced about the area. "Yes, for now, at least. I'll probably wish to come here again, if that would be agreeable."

"Of course, Mr. Holmes. We wish to accord you all reasonable courtesies, but I am certain that you will agree that we have covered the case thoroughly thus far."

"No doubt," said Holmes, "but I hope you will humour me a bit."

Lestrade smiled amiably. "Thus do we ever." He called to the policeman guarding the site to remind him that no one was to enter the area. The officer acknowledged the order and said that he would pass on the instructions to avoid compromising the scene. On the way to the morgue Holmes and Lestrade discussed the case.

"Lestrade, I believe you said that no knife was found."

"Yes, we assume the attacker took it with him. We have found no other weapons, but the snow makes it very difficult to be certain at this point."

"But you're sure that Officer McConnell was stabbed?" asked Holmes.

Lestrade looked out and said, "We've arrived; you can decide for yourself."

The two men entered the grim building, and Lestrade led Holmes immediately to the examination room. During the inspection Holmes noticed that the victim had no injuries to his hands, which suggested that his killer's attack had not been protracted. But it was clear that under the circumstances the unfortunate McConnell's neck wound had been necessarily fatal.

Holmes bent over and examined the wound closely, then straightened up. "Lestrade, do you find that wound remarkable in any way?"

Lestrade shrugged and shook his head. "No, Mr. Holmes, I see nothing unusual about it. Should I?"

"But what sort of knife would make a wound like that? Notice that it would seem to have been done by a round object, not a flat one such as a knife's blade."

Lestrade bent over and examined the wound. "Well, perhaps. Maybe the killer twisted the knife."

Holmes shook his head. "No, I can't see that as having produced what we see here."

"Well, Mr. Holmes, just what do you suggest?"

"I'm not certain, but I'd like to do some searching at the scene again."

"Certainly," said Lestrade. "But I think that one can complicate investigations by letting the imagination have too free a rein."

"Nevertheless! With your indulgence. *Informed* imagination can be essential." As Holmes scanned the body for any clues it might offer, he said softly. "I recall that he was right-handed."

"You knew him?"

Holmes nodded. "I've seen him two or three times briefly." He examined the body's right hand closely. "Yes, I thought I recalled that he smoked cigars." Bending down and sniffing the clothing, he added, "Probably quite a lot of them."

"We found several in his topcoat," said Lestrade. He walked over to a box from which he retrieved four cigars and held them up. "Here they are. Are they important?"

Holmes took the cigars and examined them. "Perhaps; we shall see." He handed them back and, with a smile, said, "Well, Lestrade, with your permission I'd like to take another look in St. James's Park."

As the two men left the building, Holmes casually asked Lestrade whether anything besides cigars was found on the dead policeman.

Lestrade smiled archly. "Well, Mr. Holmes, we found the usual personal items—and several letters."

"Have you determined that these letters have any significance for this case?"

"Nothing definite, yet, but we're still checking one avenue. In fact, now that you mention it, Mr. Holmes, they were written by a recent client of yours. At least I understand he was your client."

"Indeed? And who would that be?"

"Why, none other than Mr. Oscar Wilde."

Inside the carriage on the return to the crime scene Holmes asked whether he might be permitted to see the letters that McConnell had been carrying.

"I think that could be arranged," said Lestrade with a touch of amusement in his voice. He reached inside his topcoat and brought out four letters which he handed to Holmes. A quick glance revealed that they were private letters written by Wilde to Lord Alfred Douglas.

"Lestrade, would it be possible to let me examine these overnight?"

"Well, it would probably be frowned upon by my superiors, but I think I can trust you with their safety. After all, any light that you might be able to throw on this case would certainly help Her Majesty's government see that justice is done." Lestrade then added with some emphasis, "We would certainly expect you to apprise us of any connection your client, Mr. Wilde, might have with our officer's death."

"Of course."

Back at the crime scene, with the advantage of late-morning sunshine, a more careful search of the area promised to be useful and revealing. Holmes first turned to the two pairs of footprints entering the area from the street, for they showed a different quality from the confused mass of prints around where the body had lain. He next walked slowly across the ground traversed by the tracks and to where they apparently stopped. It was quite close to where the policeman had met his end, and Holmes began a careful search in the snow. At one point he exclaimed, "Aha!" Lestrade looked around and walked over to find Holmes digging with his index finger in the snow. He brought up a partially smoked cigar.

"Well, Mr. Holmes! What have you there?"

"Lestrade, unless I'm mistaken, this was Officer McConnell's last cigar. He must have been sufficiently sure of his companion to continue smoking when they arrived here. In fact, it is a fair assumption that the two were acquainted. Also, his companion had to have been several inches shorter than the officer. The other person's tracks suggest he had to struggle to keep up with Officer McConnell."

"How do you come to that conclusion, Mr. Holmes?"

"Observe the length of both men's strides. We know McConnell's height, which is at least six feet; and his companion's stride and prints suggest not more than about three or four inches over five feet. At times the shorter person's footprints are impressed over the officer's, as though he was at least occasionally following. I shall be interested in what conclusions your man Culbertson has reached."

"But how," asked Lestrade, "can you be sure that these prints were not made by the investigators?"

Holmes stooped down and pointed to some of the prints. "Fortunately for our work, last night's heavier snow later turned into a much lighter accumulation. Observe how the earlier snow has left much less evidence of the prints made by the two men late last night." He got up and walked over to the later prints made by the several investigators. Stopping and pointing down, he showed Lestrade that the later prints were much more distinct.

Lestrade looked pensive and murmured, "Well, I shall say only: *important if true.*"

"Of course; these are all hypotheses. But now let me do a bit more checking. I'd like to find a weapon if one is here."

With that he walked slowly over the ground, all the while searching for any significant signs. Presently he noticed a slight bulge in the accumulated snow several feet from where the body had been found and quite close to the row of shrubbery. With great care Holmes gently worked his hand under the bulge and felt the edge of something. He carefully cleared the snow away from what proved to be a knife with a blade of nearly five inches and a handle slightly shorter. Holmes held it up, carefully taking it by the tip of the blade and the end of the handle.

Having carefully observed all that Holmes was doing, Lestrade called out: "Well, Mr. Holmes, you have made an important discovery."

Holmes looked at Lestrade and then back at the item in his hands. "Yes, it's a sort of boot knife, I believe. Did you find a sheath on McConnell's body?"

"No, nothing of that sort."

"Then it may well be somewhere around here."

"We shall search for it, Mr. Holmes. Meanwhile, let me have the knife."

Holmes laid the knife gently back on the snow, then reached inside his coat and produced a cloth pouch. "Lestrade, let's put the knife into this to protect it for the present."

"Why? It's almost certainly the murder weapon and must be kept as evidence."

Holmes shook his head. "I would stake my reputation on its *not* being the weapon that killed Officer McConnell." He looked closely at the knife and said, "Indeed, there appears to be little blood on it, nothing like the amount that the neck wound should have caused. But that can all be ascertained later. Meanwhile, I urge you to protect this knife from being handled by anyone until it can be examined closely."

"May I ask why?"

"Fingerprints."

Lestrade rolled his eyes upward in a gesture of helpless frustration. Then, looking at the knife, he exclaimed: "Fingerprints? I don't see anything on it! And what if there are fingerprints? What would that prove?"

"Are you familiar with Sir Francis Galton?"

Lestrade pondered impatiently for a moment. "I don't think so. Should I be?"

"He has done a great deal of work studying fingerprints as a means of identification."

"And so?"

"Three years ago he published a book on the subject. In it he asserts that no two sets of fingerprints are the same, and that a person's prints remain the same through life." Holmes put the knife into the protective pouch, then rose and handed it to Lestrade. "All I ask is that you handle this gently and let no one touch it until it has been thoroughly tested by Galton's methods."

Reluctantly and somewhat gingerly Lestrade took the covered knife. "Should I be handling it?"

"So long as you keep it in the pouch and avoid excessive pressure, it should be safe. But we now need to do further searching. A sheath is probably around here somewhere, and very possibly a second weapon."

For several minutes the two men carefully searched the general area but without success. Then Holmes, with signs of frustration on his face, let his eyes rest upon the hedgerow and its protective wrought-iron railing. Suddenly he exclaimed, "Interesting!"

A startled Lestrade looked at him and followed his gaze. "What do you see?"

"These!" said Holmes, and he walked to the tangled, damaged shrubbery and mass of broken icicles. Picking up a frozen spike, he held it up for the inspector to see. "Lestrade, I'd bet this could make a very impressive wound." He grasped it as a dagger and made an upward thrust.

Lestrade looked not entirely convinced. "But wouldn't it shatter?"

"I think not, especially if the user thrust it straight at his victim, and into soft flesh." He handed it to Lestrade. "Check that piece of ice—its shape and length—its solidity. Don't you agree that you wouldn't care to be on the receiving end of that?"

Lestrade held the icicle and looked at it with raised eyebrows. "Yes, I daresay that it might become a lethal weapon."

Holmes glanced at the site of the struggle, and murmured, "It certainly could if someone were unarmed and in mortal danger." Then, almost as though talking to himself, Holmes added softly, "And especially if he found himself on the ground, and an attacker hovering above him."

"Indeed," said Lestrade as he concentrated on the area toward which Holmes was gesturing. "And if the one attacked thrust it into the other's neck."

"Quite so, Lestrade, one of our most vulnerable spots, a narrow area of vital arteries and veins, to say nothing of the trachea." Holmes pondered for several moments. "Let's consider the possibility that your officer was the aggressor and that whoever was with him was caught by surprise. Then, let's hypothesise that the other person had no weapon and was knocked into the shrubbery and the ice formations. In such a situation a quick glance might well have suggested a large icicle as a weapon."

Lestrade nodded thoughtfully. "That certainly is not implausible. The wound on the officer's body is consistent with a blow from something such as this." He held it up, made a grimace, and tossed it aside.

Holmes paused, glanced about himself, and became thoughtful. "What if we could find the exact piece of ice that did this? In this temperature it might well be still intact." He began looking carefully at and around the spot where McConnell had fallen. Lestrade joined him in a search that lasted about ten minutes.

"Mr. Holmes, I believe there's something right here." The inspector carefully removed the snow from the object, just under the snow's surface, which proved to be about a seven-inch section of an icicle.

"Excellent, Lestrade, I think you've found what we need. And look at that footprint. Someone barely missed stepping on it." Holmes examined the icicle more closely and then the snow where it had lain. "Lestrade, unless I err, there are traces of blood here. What do you think?"

"It would certainly seem that you're right." Lestrade shook his head and murmured, "Unfortunately, we are not going to be able to preserve it." He looked over at the officer on guard. "Officer Bennett, would you come here?"

Bennett walked smartly over to the inspector. "Yes, sir?"

"Mr. Holmes and I have found what appears to be the object that was used to kill McConnell. But since it *is* ice, we aren't going to be able to preserve it. I'd like you to be prepared to vouch for our having found it and for the site of the discovery."

The officer stooped down and made a close examination of the icicle and its position. "Anything that you want me to particularly notice, sir?"

"Just recall how everything looks, Bennett," said the inspector, "where it lies, and how it looks. Also, observe the slight trace of blood at the spot and even on the ice itself." Lestrade looked over at Holmes and suggested that they might manage to collect at least a little of the blood in order to prove that it indeed *was* blood.

At first Lestrade suspected that Oscar Wilde, even if not the murderer, was somehow involved in the death of Officer McConnell. Holmes was aware of this but was certain that once he had explained all his evidence, Wilde would probably be cleared of any suspicion. Holmes testified before an inquest and argued convincingly that the unknown person's tracks in the snow could not have been made by a man taller than about five-feet-four inches tall. Wilde was at least as tall as McConnell. Furthermore, Holmes's demonstration of the new science of fingerprint analysis showed that the only prints on the knife were the victim's. In addition, a carrying sheath later found on the scene had the initials *SM* written on it in ink. Officer McConnell had almost certainly been armed with it, and further evidence suggested that he probably had been the aggressor. The letters from Wilde to Douglas that were found on the body of the deceased could not yet be explained, but the police were inclined to remove Wilde's name from the list of suspects.

Holmes, however, knew that he needed to inform Wilde of all that had happened and to ask whether the writer could help clarify the unknown aspects of the case. In light of Wilde's eminence, Lestrade was content to let Holmes question him first. Fortunately for Wilde's family, Holmes was able to talk with Wilde at his temporary rooms at the Avondale Hotel.

"Mr. Holmes, I hope you know that I had no connection with this tragic event."

"I'm convinced of that, Mr. Wilde, and I've given my reasons to the police. But they still don't know who the other person was, nor do we know why the policeman, Sean McConnell, had letters you had written."

"Perhaps," said Wilde, "I can suggest something relevant. And in telling you this, I hope you will, if at all possible, treat the information as confidential."

Holmes nodded. "Of course, so long as the police don't regard you as a suspect."

"Do you think they are likely to do so?"

"Not from what has been discovered thus far."

Wilde had already told Holmes about the several young men who had recently attempted without success to blackmail him. Now Wilde explained that a policeman had called on him to ask whether he knew why McConnell would have been carrying letters that Wilde had written to Alfred Douglas. This prompted Wilde to go immediately to talk with an acquaintance named Alfred Taylor, who lived in Little College Street. Taylor knew some of these young blackmailers, and in the course of the conversation told Wilde that one of the men, Dennis Cassidy, had quite recently sustained some minor injuries to his hands, face, and back. When asked about them, the young man had been evasive and clearly uncomfortable. Holmes wrote down the young man's name, as well as Alfred Taylor's name and address.

Through information provided by Taylor, Holmes found Cassidy and persuaded him to tell what had happened between him and Sean McConnell.

"Young man, I think your only choice in this case is to explain frankly to me and to the police what happened that night." Holmes looked sternly at Cassidy and lifted a warning finger. "If you work with me and tell me exactly what happened, I think I can help you."

Cassidy swore that he had never seen McConnell before that night, though he had heard earlier that the officer was working for the Marquess of Queensberry and was interested in having certain letters that Wilde had written to Lord Alfred Douglas.

"Did you know Lord Alfred?"

Cassidy hesitated, then admitted that he had seen both Wilde and Douglas a few times at Alfred Taylor's. "But I never wanted to do Mr. Wilde no harm. He was always a kind gentleman, he was."

Holmes looked keenly at Cassidy. "Did you ever spend any time with Mr. Wilde?" The young man looked unsure how to reply, and Holmes said, "I think you know what I mean."

"No, sir, there ain't never been nothing like that between him and me, not *no* time."

"And you never tried to blackmail Mr. Wilde?" asked Holmes.

"I *never* did but some of them other blokes did try. But when they tried to make Mr. Wilde buy his letters back, he just made fun of 'em. I said they ought to leave Mr. Wilde alone."

"And how did they respond to this?"

"They was pretty hot and said that if Mr. Wilde wouldn't pay for 'em, Lord Queensberry would. They said a policeman was working for His Lordship and would pay good money for them letters."

"And what did you do then?"

"I got several of the letters and was going to give 'em back to Mr. Wilde. But Officer McConnell found out about it and stopped me in St. James's Park."

"What time was this?"

"About eleven o'clock."

"In the evening, you mean?"

"Yes, sir."

"And what happened when you two met?"

"Well," said Cassidy, "it was real cold and I was walking along at a right brisk clip, when this big bloke come up to me. He was smoking a cigar and asked me if I'd like one. I told him no thanks. He said his name was McConnell and that he was a policeman, though he didn't have no uniform on. He said it sort of threatening like. He then said he was working for Lord Queensberry, who was interested in the letters I was carrying."

"Did he say how he knew you had the letters?"

"No, sir, but I suppose Allen and some of the others told 'im."

"All right. Then what happened?"

"He said we needed to talk about it, and he told me to step off the street and move to a place where the street lamp wouldn't make us so visible. He said the letters needed to be turned over to the police and that he was supposed to get 'em. I took 'em out of my pocket and held 'em up, and said I had 'em and they was going back to Mr. Wilde. McConnell then said that the Marquess of Queensberry would pay me good money for the letters. I told him I liked Mr. Wilde and wasn't interested in selling the letters to nobody."

"How did he take that information?"

"Oh, he was really mad and started threatening to arrest me. Then he lunged at me and snatched the letters out of my hand. I tried to grab 'em back, and he started pushing me, and he slapped me two or three times. I couldn't get the letters back before he put 'em inside his coat. He lunged at me but I managed to back away from 'im. But before I could run from 'im, he took out a knife and began to walk toward me. I backed away from 'im and tripped on something. Before I knew it, the copper was crouching over me and he raised his knife over me. I was trying to keep 'im away; and when he brought the knife down, I managed to dodge it, but it cut a small gash on my hand. I tried to roll out from under 'im, and it was then that I saw some big icicles that had broke off when I fell against the iron railing. They looked almost like daggers, so I picked one up and slammed it into the officer's neck. He yelled and fell partly on top of me, but I got myself free and ran. I didn't even try to get the letters back, and I left his knife where he dropped it."

Holmes later told Lestrade what Dennis Cassidy had said and that it accorded with all the evidence. Cassidy told his account to the police, who concluded that the young man had acted in self-defense and that Officer Sean McConnell had demeaned himself and brought about his own death. There was some question about whether the police should arrest Queensberry; but it was decided that, technically at least, he had broken no law.

The tragic incident, however, had the effect of warning Wilde that his enemy was using some extraordinary methods to get information about him. Unfortunately, he did not take the warning as seriously as he ought to have. At a time of threatening crisis, he and Lord Alfred decided to be away from London. Algiers seemed to offer a respite from the hell that London was becoming.

Chapter 6

A few days later Wilde and his wife were discussing his imminent trip to Algiers with Bosie Douglas. They chatted in a small downstairs room of the Wildes' Tite Street home. It was the room in which Wilde preferred to do his writing rather than in his study on the floor above. Here, his desk that had once belonged to Thomas Carlyle provided his favorite working surface. A statue of Hermes stood guard, and pictures by well-known artists adorned the walls.

Constance, her face registering sadness and frustration, asked, "How long do you think you'll be gone, Oscar?"

"My dear, probably not more than two or three weeks. It will take all that time to get sufficient rest from the work I've had to do on my two plays."

"I hope it will be no longer than that," she said softly.

"It must *not* be longer. *Earnest* will open in the middle of next month, and I'll have to be here while George Alexander is still rehearsing."

"That's good to know," she replied. "Bosie, will you stay there that long, too?"

"I suppose so, Constance, but I may have to get back a little sooner."

At this point the Wildes' two little sons entered, even as they were in the midst of an argument. Vyvyan complained that Cyril had taken one of his toys and wouldn't give it back.

Wilde looked sternly at Cyril and said, "Cyril, return Vyvyan's toy and go immediately and ask God to make you a better boy."

After the boys had left, Wilde turned to Bosie and said: "The other night I was reading my sons a story about naughty boys who made their mothers cry. Vyvyan turned to me and asked, 'And what about naughty papas who don't come home until late at night and make the mothers cry even more?'" He looked sheepishly at Constance and said, "My dear, I suppose I certainly am guilty of that. I'm so sorry and am fully determined to be a better husband and father."

Constance made an effort to smile when she replied, "Oh, Oscar, I know you mean well. Besides, I've become reconciled to having to share you with the world. But I do hope that Algiers won't keep you longer than two weeks."

"I will do my best not to stay beyond that. But I begin to think that Algiers is the Lotus Land where Odysseus visited and where the inhabitants fed on lotus fruit that erased all memory of their pasts. That's probably where all writers of memoirs go to do their work." He looked wistful as he added, "Perhaps I shall find a way to forget all the unpleasant things and remember only the nice ones, especially those that have never happened." He stepped into the hall and called up to the boys' room: "Cyril, did you pray God to make you a better boy?"

Cyril's voice came back, "No, Father, I asked God to make *Vyvyan* a better boy."

Wilde returned to the room and said, "I do believe Cyril has already learned one of the main keys to success."

Elsewhere in London the Marquess of Queensberry read the day's newspaper in his hotel. At one point he threw the paper to the floor and made a sound of disgust. One of his cronies who sat nearby reading a magazine looked up. "What's wrong now?"

"My man McConnell's dead and it appears the police don't think anyone's responsible for it. Wilde's the one to blame, even if he himself didn't kill McConnell. And I need to get those letters the police found on him."

"Why don't you forget Wilde and stop letting him ruin your life?"

"Like hell! I'm going to ruin *his* life!"

"Why? What good will that do?"

"A lot more than doing nothing!"

"All right—so what happens now?"

The marquess didn't reply immediately; he just stared ahead. Finally, he looked at his companion. "He has a new play that's due to open about the middle of February. I'd give anything to see that its first night is a disaster. It would be wonderful to make that first night the play's last—and his, too."

"What play is this?"

"Oh, the importance of something or other." Queensberry chuckled bitterly. "Ha! It's a comedy! Well, I'll give the first-night audience something to really laugh about."

"And what will that be."

"Not sure yet, but I'm working on it."

"But you couldn't do anything to stop his last play."

Queensberry sneered. "I wasn't trying to. I just put out that report to scare them."

"You think they'll let you in?"

"I've reserved two tickets."

"Two? Why two?"

"In case I take a good bodyguard with me."

Early in February Wilde returned to London from Algiers. At once he began haunting the St. James's Theatre and, in his customary manner, pestering the cast during their rehearsals. Someone passed George Alexander one day and said to him, "I understand that you're rehearsing with the author's assistance."

Alexander laughed and replied, "No, with his interference."

On one occasion during a practice Wilde corrected an actor about the delivery of a line. The actor said testily, "I know my lines, Mr. Wilde."

"Ah, yes, but do you know mine?" said Wilde.

When someone asked him whether he regarded actors as creative artists, he replied, "Terribly creative, terribly creative."

Wilde's concern for the integrity of his plays was not unlike that of a father for his children. And if possible, his anxiety about *The Importance of Being Earnest* was even greater than he had felt for his first three comedies. It was as though he sensed that this fourth comedy rose to a new level, that it was indeed his best. Perhaps he sensed also that it might be his last.

He would often sit just offstage as the cast rehearsed. During one rehearsal of *Earnest* a cast member delivered a line which threw everyone on stage into a frenzy of laughter. One of the actresses happened to glance over at the author sitting there and glumly observing the scene. She walked over to him and asked why he seemed so disconsolate.

Wilde looked up at her and said with feeling, "They are laughing at my lines, actually laughing."

"Well, Mr. Wilde, I should think that you'd be pleased at that. What a compliment to your wonderful abilities."

"Yes, yes," said Wilde, "but I never can get people to take me seriously." He looked off into the distance and added, "What do you think the public will say after this about my blank verse?"

She looked disappointed. "Do you think we are rendering your lines badly?"

He straightened up in his chair. "No, I won't say that, but I do wish that the cast would take me seriously and not let the audience know that they think the lines are funny."

"How should we do that?"

"By delivering the amusing lines straight-faced and matter-of-factly." He picked up a copy of the script. "Look there, below the title. Do you see the subtitle?"

The actress stared at it and then read aloud, "*A Trivial Comedy for Serious People.*" She looked at him and admitted that she had never before thought much about that.

"I fear," said Wilde wryly, "that even Mr. Alexander has not thought much about it, or at least has not taken it quite literally."

George Alexander strolled over. "Oscar, is there a problem?" Wilde explained to him what he had just said to the actress, and the actor-manager mused about it for a moment. He thought the point an interesting one and gathered all the cast to explain that he wanted them to start delivering all their lines with serious faces except where the script clearly called for the actor to do otherwise.

Alexander had already been warned that the Marquess of Queensberry was planning to create a disturbance on opening night, and the theatre manager immediately cancelled the peer's reservation. The enraged marquess, accompanied by a henchman, headed to the St. James's Theatre on the night of February 14; but both the police and the weather were working to thwart Queensberry's plans. One of London's worst snowstorms in years was creating difficulties for both pedestrians and carriages. Nevertheless, a very fashionable crowd of theatre-goers made their way to the gala opening night.

Sherlock Holmes and Dr. Watson were among the throng. Holmes surveyed the general scene as their hansom neared the theatre. "Watson, if Queensberry expects to disrupt the opening, I think he must now realise that it's not going to be easy. Well, if I know anything about the man, he'll regard all this as simply making his mischief all the more satisfying." Holmes pointed toward the entrance to the theatre. "I see that the police are already on hand. Look over there—and down there—and on that corner. It seems that the police have every entry covered."

"Indeed! And even the weather seems to have turned against Queensberry." Watson looked out and saw that their cabbie was going to have to make a slow way up to the entrance. "Holmes, why don't we get out here and walk the rest of the way?"

"Good idea." Holmes called to the driver to let them out. He paid their fares, and the two men stepped into a heavy accumulation of snow and made their way to the entrance.

There, a policeman recognized Holmes and Watson and spoke to them. "Mr. Holmes and Dr. Watson, good to see you. I think you'll have a really good play tonight."

"Well, Allbrook, let's hope that all the acting will be on the stage," said Holmes with a knowing look at the officer.

"Oh, don't you worry about that, Mr. Holmes. Queensberry won't be able to get into this place. Mr. Alexander has given us complete liberty to do whatever is necessary. You'll be able to just sit back and enjoy what I hear is a really good show."

"Will you see it, Allbrook?" asked Watson.

"Oh, not tonight, sir. I'll see it in good time. So, you two just relax and don't worry."

Outside, Queensberry and his bodyguard, Bledsoe, alighted from a hansom and entered the theatre. While his companion dropped back and waited, Queensberry, with a package under one arm, walked over to the ticket office to claim his two re-served tickets. Before the person on duty could reply, however, a theatre employee intruded.

"Lord Queensberry, I'm sorry but all tickets have been sold."

"That's ridiculous!" shouted Queensberry. "All these other people have been getting them."

"Those tickets had been previously reserved; they were simply picking them up."

"But I reserved mine, too!" exclaimed Queensberry.

"I'm sorry, Lord Queensberry, but there are no available tickets."

By this time, two policemen had moved nearer the angry marquess He glanced uneasily at them and in the distance saw several other men who seemed to be watching him very closely.

He glared angrily at all of them, then turned briskly and, motioning to Bledsoe, returned to the street in a foul temper. The two stood there uncertain what to do next. Upon Bledsoe's suggestion that such a building had to have several entrances, Queensberry nodded and, followed by his bodyguard, started to the corner. From the corner they could see someone standing near a side entrance. In an effort not to attract attention, they strolled casually toward the door; but as soon as they reached it, they realised that the person standing there was another policeman. With typical bravado Queensberry walked up to the officer, who did not recognise the marquess. The latter was doing his best to hide his anger.

"May I help you gentlemen?" asked the officer.

"Yes, officer, I have a package that I'd like to deliver to Mr. Wilde.

"I'm sorry, sir, but my orders are to let no one pass into the theatre."

Queensberry tried to frame his facial expression to show extreme disappointment. "Well, could you at least deliver this yourself, or else ask someone else to do so?"

The officer turned and stuck his head inside the building and called to a young stagehand, who came to the door. "Do you know who Mr. Wilde is?"

"Yeah! Who don't?"

"Well," said the officer, "I'd like you to take something to him." With that the policeman took the package from Queensberry and handed it to the young man. "Be sure you put this right into Mr. Wilde's hands."

As the young man took the package, he looked curiously at it. "What's in it?"

"Don't worry about that. Just hand it directly to Mr. Wilde. You understand?"

"Oh, sure. Right away."

The officer turned back to Queensberry and Bledsoe. "That ought to get it to him, gentlemen."

Queensberry nodded mechanically. "Come on, Bledsoe, let's get out of here. In frustration he started walking quickly back toward the theatre's entrance, all the while grumbling and shaking his fist in the air. Every so often he yelled about the theatre's manager, about Wilde and Wilde's play, about the actors, the government, the Prime Minister, and several other groups and individuals, all of whom he vowed to thrash.

Oh! he had planned a theatrical evening for this occasion! He'd have shown the audience some *real* acting, some moving declamation that would have made theatrical history. He hadn't been able even to deliver personally his bunch of vegetables. Wouldn't that congratulatory *bouquet* have been something to set before the cast! And, oh! how he had practiced precisely the speech he had intended to make after throwing it. His enraged mood and furious walking caused him to slip on the snow in a most undignified manner and land on his seat. Bledsoe helped him to his feet, but now there was physical discomfort to match his rage.

They would pay! thought Queensberry as he signaled a four-wheeler and gave the cab driver an address. For several moments the two men sat in silence as the cab took them to Queensberry's club. Then Bledsoe broke the silence.

"So, what do you do now?"

"Get even with those bastards!"

"In what way?"

"I don't know, but I'll do something." After a pause he added, "And it'll be decisive!"

The evening proved to be a legend in theatrical history. The audience were dressed in their finest and most stylish attires. The interior of the theatre contrasted most agreeably with the terrible weather outside; and for a small group of informed persons, the presence of policemen afforded an extra feeling of snug security. George Alexander could be not only relieved but also sensible of his theatre's good fortune in producing this unique new play. And the production *was* a grand success. It was a flawless performance by the cast and, as the author put it, also by the audience.

There were loud calls for Wilde. But the playwright declined to appear before the curtain. He had spent almost the entire evening backstage, for he was becoming increasingly apprehensive about his situation. His wit, however, never deserted him; and when, after the final curtain, Alexander asked him what he thought of the first performance, Wilde said: "My dear Alec, it was charming, quite charming. And, do you know, from time to time I was reminded of a play I once wrote myself called *The Importance of Being Earnest*." Alec's startled expression brought a laugh from Wilde, and a sincere reassurance: "My dear fellow, I was trying to be funny. You and the cast have performed beautifully. I could not ask for a better representation of what I had in mind when I wrote the play."

The following day Holmes and Watson were in their home. One of Holmes's clients had just left, and the two men were surprised to hear loud, unfamiliar voices in the entrance hall. They heard also their landlady's emphatic statement that the two visitors should not enter Mr. Holmes' residence without his consent. Despite Mrs. Hudson's protests, Holmes and

Watson heard heavy footsteps on the stairway. Then, through the suddenly opened door came two men, and both Holmes and Watson rose from their chairs.

"Lord Queensberry," said Holmes dryly, "you seem to have a very remarkable talent for unwelcome entrances."

Watson's startled look momentarily caught Queensberry's attention. He sneered and asked sarcastically, "Well, who do we have here?" Turning to his companion, he exclaimed, "Bledsoe, London seems to be full of 'em!"

"Indeed it does," said Holmes evenly. "I shall have to inform Scotland Yard that the city apparently is experiencing an epidemic of trespassing. Watson, let me introduce to you the Marquess of Queensberry, the person that our client has very aptly called 'the most infamous brute in London.'"

Watson looked uncertainly at Holmes, then back at the marquess, and then moved over to a desk in which he kept a handgun. He unobtrusively opened the drawer and glanced down at the weapon.

"Lord Queensberry," said Holmes, "I would be entirely justified in throwing you out of my home. However, if you wish to say something pertinent, and in a civil manner, I shall be very willing to listen. Otherwise, I must demand that you leave."

After a moment, Queensberry asked angrily, "May we sit down?"

"If you can control yourself."

After all four men had seated themselves, Holmes spoke first. "And now, what is it you wish to say to me?"

"I want you to stop working with Oscar Wilde against me and giving him advice."

"Lord Queensberry, my helping Mr. Wilde has nothing to do with you, unless you make it so."

"Well, you've been much in his company the last few weeks. And you were in his house when I was there recently."

"As I just said, he sought my help on a matter totally unrelated to you. I have successfully completed my investigation for him, and he has been kind enough to provide Dr. Watson and me with tickets to his two recent plays." Holmes smiled and added blandly, "I hope, by the way, you won't miss those plays, for both are excellent."

"I certainly have no intention of seeing those plays or anything else that Oscar Wilde has anything to do with!" exclaimed Queensberry. "The man is a public menace. He engages in the most disgraceful conduct."

"I have seen nothing of his behaving in any such way. And I've *heard* nothing about any disgraceful behaviour except from rumourmongers."

Rising from his chair, Queensberry shouted, "He is not a gentleman!"

"And you, sir, are obviously no judge." With a mocking smile, Holmes added, "At any rate, I've certainly heard nothing of Mr. Wilde's entering persons' homes uninvited."

"I have good reason to do that! Besides, that's a minor matter."

"At present it is a very important matter to me." Holmes rose from his chair. "If this is all you have to say, Marquess, I must order you to leave my home."

Watson spoke up. "After all, to quote one of those wonderful lines from Mr. Wilde's latest play, 'No doubt you have many other calls of a similar character to make in the neighbourhood.'"

Queensberry's face reddened, and he sputtered inarticulately. He turned to his companion who stood up and started to walk toward Holmes. Holmes's body tensed, and Watson reached down and placed his hand on his pistol.

At this point the door opened and a policeman entered, with a terrified Mrs. Hudson peeping around the opened door.

"Ah, Sergeant Gresham," exclaimed Holmes, "how opportune your visit is!" "Lord Queensberry and his friend were just leaving, and under the circumstances they probably would be very happy to have safe escort."

The furious peer seemed uncertain what to say or to do. He started to speak to the policeman, turned back toward Holmes as though to make a parting comment, and finally turned toward his companion and motioned with his head that they should leave.

After the unwelcome visitors had left, Mrs. Hudson entered the room almost in tears. "Mr. Holmes and Dr. Watson, I hope I did the right thing. But that man was so rude when I answered the door! And from what I could hear from the hall I was afraid that he might cause harm to both of you." Shaking her head she exclaimed, "I didn't know what else to do but run out and summon a policeman!"

"Calm yourself, dear Mrs. Hudson. You did well."

"Indeed, you did," added Watson. "That is one of the crudest and most outrageous men in London. In England! You probably helped avoid a very violent scene."

As Holmes and Watson were later discussing the recent, unwelcome visitation, Watson happened to suggest that Queensberry was of the same mold as Professor Moriarty and Colonel Moran, with whom Holmes had contended in recent years.

"Oh, very superficially, perhaps," said Holmes. "But both Moriarty and Moran were far cleverer and more dangerous than

Queensberry. Queensberry has all the requisites for successful criminality except intelligence."

"And perhaps bravery," added Watson.

"Indeed! I think our marquess is essentially a coward."

His failure to gain entrance at the St. James's Theatre, as well as his aborted visit to 221-B Baker Street, left Queensberry a very frustrated and angry man. He fretted for a day or two; and on the following Monday, accompanied by his friend Bledsoe, he betook himself to the Albemarle Club, where Wilde had membership. Bledsoe would serve as his witness, for he was determined to precipitate a legal confrontation with the man whom he now blamed for all his troubles. Queensberry and Bledsoe entered the club and went over to a hall porter, whom the marquess addressed.

"I understand that Oscar Wilde is a member here."

"Yes, sir. But I believe he's not here at present."

"Well, that's not important. I'd like you to give him something from me when he is next here."

"Of course, sir."

Queensberry took out one of his visiting cards. On it he wrote: "For Oscar Wilde posing somdomite." Perhaps his angry haste caused not only the misspelling but also a failure to write what might have been a more legally-defensible *For Oscar Wilde posing as a sodomite*. Nevertheless, presumably like Pontius Pilate, he had written what he had written, and that ended the matter. "Give that to Oscar Wilde," said Queensberry to the porter as he handed him the card unenclosed and open for anyone to see.

"Yes, sir." The porter looked at the card; and though unsure what the rather poor handwriting said, was reasonably certain that it was not complimentary. He then carefully enclosed it in one of the club's envelopes, on the front of which he wrote "Oscar Wilde, Esq."

Meanwhile, Wilde did not go to his club for several days. He had been staying at the Avondale Hotel in Piccadilly, not only as a refuge from the discomfort he felt at home but also as a place where he could try to make sense of the wreck that his life had become. What was worse, an unwelcome Bosie Douglas imposed himself upon Wilde and proceeded to run up a heavy bill. Bosie's request that Wilde also pay for one of Douglas' young friends to stay there was too much for even the long-suffering Wilde. An indignant Bosie left with his friend for another hotel and wrote several bitter letters to Wilde during the next several days. This helped persuade Wilde to seek the relative quiet of the Albemarle Club. When he arrived, one of the club's employees handed him the card that Queensberry had left several days before.

Wilde opened the covering envelope and managed to make out the gist of Queensberry's scribbled note. He asked the porter whether the marquess had put the card into the envelope and was told he had not. Angry and uneasy Wilde immediately went to a desk, grabbed a piece of stationery, and wrote a message to Robert Ross: "Since I saw you, something has happened. Bosie's father has left a card at my club with hideous words on it. I don't see anything now but a criminal prosecution." He asked Ross to meet him the next day at the hotel and, if possible, to bring Bosie Douglas. In addition, he suggested that Ross try to contact Holmes and Watson to see whether they could join them.

From this point events happened quickly. Disregarding the advice of his best-informed friends and acquaintances, Wilde went rashly forward by swearing out a warrant against the

Marquess of Queensberry for libel. Bosie Douglas was using Wilde to attack his father, and Queensberry was attacking Wilde to punish his son. And Wilde was allowing it to happen.

The next several weeks were difficult for almost everyone, none more so than Constance Wilde. Two days before the trial began, Wilde accompanied his wife and Bosie Douglas to a restaurant and then to see *The Importance of Being Earnest*. As they entered the theatre, they were met by George Alexander.

"Oscar, I don't think you ought to be here. People will probably think it in bad taste, just at this time."

"Are you accusing all these others of bad taste for seeing the play? I'd think it in bad taste if they went to some other play."

"Do be serious," said Alexander as he nervously glanced about the foyer.

"Then you mustn't be funny."

Alexander showed angry frustration. "Will you take some advice?"

"Certainly, if it's advice I like. But it's a dangerous thing to give advice, Alec; and giving good advice can be fatal."

"*Do be serious!* I want you to withdraw from the case and go abroad."

"But, Alec, I've already been twice abroad during the past several months. Another such trip would look like indecision."

"Oh, you're impossible!"

"No, not impossible, my dear fellow. Improbable, perhaps."

Wilde's party did see the play, through all of which Wilde laughed heartily. But Alexander's good advice, which Wilde had received also from several others, was ignored. And when the Wildes left the theatre, Constance had tears in her eyes.

Wilde's prosecution of Queensberry was the sensation of London society. Representing Wilde was Sir Edward Clarke, one of England's most respected barristers. Defending Queensberry was Edward Carson, a relatively young but ambitious and upward-moving attorney who had been a schoolmate of Wilde's at Trinity College, Dublin. In Carson's early cross-examination of Wilde, the playwright held his own, especially when Carson tried to use Wilde's literary works against him. The lawyer spent much cross-examination on Wilde's *Picture of Dorian Gray*.

"You are of opinion, I believe," said Carson, "that there is no such thing as an immoral book?"

"Yes. In writing a play or a book I am concerned entirely with literature; that is, with art. I aim not at doing good or evil, but in trying to make a thing that will have some quality or form of beauty or wit."

Carson continued: "Then I take it that no matter how immoral a book may be, if it is well written, it is in your opinion a good book?"

"Yes."

"Then," replied Carson, "a well-written book putting forward perverted moral views may be a good book?"

"No work of art ever puts forward views," explained Wilde. "Views belong to people who are not artists."

"A perverted novel might be a good book?"

"I do not know what you mean by a perverted novel," replied Wilde.

"Then I will suggest *Dorian Gray* as open to the interpretation of being such a novel."

"That could only be to brutes and illiterates. The views of philistines on art are incalculably stupid."

Carson slyly followed this with, "An illiterate person reading *Dorian Gray* might consider it such a novel?"

"The views of illiterates on art are unaccountable."

"The majority of persons," persisted Carson, "would come under your definition of philistines and illiterates?"

"I have found wonderful exceptions."

"In your story, the affection of the painter for Dorian Gray might lead an ordinary individual to believe that it might have a certain tendency?" asked Carson.

"I have no knowledge of the views of ordinary individuals."

Carson sneeringly observed, "You did not prevent the ordinary person from buying your book, did you?"

"I have never discouraged him."

Thus for some time did Wilde fend off successfully almost every step of Carson's vigorous and able interrogation. But when Wilde's attorney discovered the depth of searching done by Queensberry's partisans and attorneys, aided by paid informants and sometimes perjured witnesses, he advised Wilde to drop his case. It meant that Queensberry's libelous accusation had been officially proved; Wilde was now subject to arrest.

The evening following the collapse of Wilde's prosecution of Queensberry, Holmes and Watson invited Robert Ross, Frank Harris, and several others to their home to discuss the appalling developments. They had learned that Wilde had been hounded out of at least one hotel, and that crowds had jeered at him and taunted him as he tried to recover his equilibrium. Several of Wilde's friends urged him to leave England for the Continent; and the authorities delayed carrying out an arrest warrant, apparently in the hope that Wilde would do just that and avoid another, more embarrassing public trial. Frank Harris mentioned that he had arranged to have a steam vessel waiting in the Thames to take Wilde quickly to France. Wilde refused the offer.

"I think Oscar is just spineless and weak-willed," said Harris; but Ross and Holmes took strong exception to this.

With some heat Ross exclaimed that it was clear that Harris did not know Wilde. Holmes, also, expressed his doubts that Harris was correct. From all he had seen of Wilde during their brief acquaintance, he was certain that the reason for his refusal to leave was something else entirely.

"I understand, for instance," said Holmes, "that Wilde's mother, Lady Wilde, has told her son that she would disown him if he left England at this time."

"That would certainly be a strong reason," said Ross, "but I think an even stronger one is that Oscar is not practical enough to realize what's in store for him. In the past he has always been able to charm people and to extricate himself from difficult predicaments. He doesn't realize that he will now be in a very different situation."

Wilde was arrested as he sat in the Cadogan Hotel. There, surrounded by several friends, he seemed listless as he sipped hock and seltzer. At some point there was a knock at the door. Two policemen were admitted, and one addressed Wilde.

"Mr. Wilde, I believe?"

"Yes."

"We are police officers and hold a warrant for your arrest."

"Oh, really?"

"I must ask you to accompany us to the police station."

"Certainly," replied Wilde. "Just let me get my overcoat and hat."

His several friends looked somber as Wilde was led outside and into a waiting carriage. During the ride to the station the officers found Wilde interesting and witty, which under the circumstances was remarkable. As they passed a popular restaurant, one of the policemen mentioned how much he would enjoy dropping in for a good meal.

"I think both of you gentlemen would find the place less than satisfactory," suggested Wilde.

"The food isn't good?" asked one officer.

"It's even worse than that," said Wilde. "It's healthful. Admittedly, the décor is remarkable and, for all I know, may taste better than the food. It could hardly be worse."

"You say so, sir? I shall certainly keep that in mind."

"Yes," said Wilde, "I understand that the owner is a former Nonconformist clergyman, who saw the light and became a restaurateur. I understand that he is unsubtle enough to brag that he went from saving souls to serving soles."

It was the end of his acclaimed and exquisite life, and one in which he had experienced one of the most brilliant and successful careers of the Victorian writers. Sadly, however, his time of eminence had been as brief as the remainder of his life would be.

At Wilde's first appearance in court as the defendant, the jury could not agree. Pending a second trial, he was granted bail, which obliged him to search for an available place to spend his brief respite. Queensberry and his minions managed to hound him out of hotels until he finally, in desperation, went to his mother's home. There he had to endure the presence of his difficult brother.

Ernest and Ada Leverson came to his rescue by offering their home as a place to await the second trial. The Leversons gathered their servants and explained that Wilde would be arriving to stay until his new trial. Ernest Leverson said: "I'm sure you all know about his present situation. Mr. Wilde needs a pleasant, comfortable, and quiet place to live before he has to endure another trial. I feel it only fair to you to explain this and to ask you now whether you think you will be able to make him feel welcome." He paused, then added: "If any of you think this would be too difficult to do, I shall understand and will pay a month's wages to anyone who prefers to be discharged."

The butler cleared his throat. "Well, sir—sir and madam—speaking for myself and I think for the rest of us—well, sir, we've most of us read the case, but we know Mr. Wilde, and we have always been proud to wait on him, and proud we shall still be, sir, if I may make so bold—we'll all of us do all we can to make the poor gentleman comfortable."

Both Leversons smiled appreciatively. Ernest looked around at the others and asked whether this was the general sense. They all nodded vigorously. The Leversons thanked all their servants and reminded them not to mention to anyone outside their home that Wilde was there. Ada and Ernest then withdrew into another room.

"Well," said Ada, "that takes care of everyone except our coachman."

Ernest nodded. "Yes, I think he sometimes tends to talk too much about his work." He mused for a moment, then said, "What say we give him a month's holiday starting right now?"

"Good idea," said Ada. "I'll hire a brougham to go over to Lady Wilde's and bring Oscar here."

Wilde soon arrived with Ada, who quickly and quietly escorted him upstairs to the nursery floor, where the harried guest had at his disposal two large rooms, a smaller one, and a bathroom. There were also for his delectation many toys scattered about. Wilde confessed to being charmed at the fanciful, innocent atmosphere.

"Sphinx, I owe you so much," said Wilde. "The situation at my mother's was very difficult. My dear brother could not resist behaving like a Nonconformist clergyman. I expect soon to hear that he has taken Holy Orders, or whatever Nonconformists call it."

"Oscar, I owe you so much, too! You are always welcome here, and I want you to feel at home. And please feel free to move about our home at your pleasure."

"You are most kind, Sphinx, but I don't wish to cause you any trouble. And I particularly don't wish to be an embarrassment to you and Ernest. I shall remain mostly in my room."

"You must not even think of that. We are not embarrassed, but indeed proud for you to be with us where we can perhaps be of some service to you." Then, to introduce a different subject, she smiled, clapped her hand, and exclaimed: "But now you must get ready for dinner. We'll start serving in about forty-five minutes."

Fully dressed, even to the flower in his buttonhole, Wilde appeared in the dining room promptly at six that evening and every evening. It was an all-too-brief respite. Once his trial began, he would have to stay again at his mother's home.

Wilde's second trial was prosecuted personally by the Solicitor-General Frank Lockwood, who performed his duty with particular zeal, relish, and bitterness. Many then, and many others since that time, have thought that the government ought to have dropped the case after the first trial's failure to get a conviction. Even Edward Carson, chief counsel for Queensberry at the latter's trial for libel, was dubious about the wisdom of trying Wilde again. He tried to dissuade Lockwood.

"Poor Wilde has suffered a great deal, Sir Frank. Can't you let up on the fellow now?"

"I dare not. If I did so, it would be said everywhere that we dropped the case to protect the several well-known persons whose names we referred to during the trial, but carefully refrained from reading out in court."

"But," said Carson, "why couldn't you just have read all those names out in court?"

"Well," said Lockwood curtly, "we did not; so that's that." With a grumble he added, "Anyway, I want to see this man Wilde punished with every weapon we have."

The prejudiced atmosphere in which the second trial was conducted made the result inevitable. Wilde was found guilty and sentenced to two years of hard labour. The judge, Mr. Justice Sir Alfred Wills, was scathing in his final statement. He relished saying that he thought the maximum sentence totally inadequate. At the pronouncement of the sentence, there were cries of "Shame" in the courtroom. Wilde turned pale, stared incredulously, and gasped out, "And I? May I say nothing, my lord?"

The judge contemptuously waved his hand to the warders to remove the prisoner, and Wilde was taken hold of just as he seemed about to collapse. His guards quickly conducted him below.

Outside the Old Bailey the news of Wilde's conviction started a modest pandemonium. Those who had witnessed the end of the trial were just coming out, and these began to mix with those who had simply milled about outside the Central Criminal Court. News of the trial's outcome quickly spread from person to person and to various other areas of the city. In very little time several newspapers appeared with dramatically large headlines announcing the sensational news.

Elsewhere in London that evening two actors, Charles Hawtrey and Charles Brookfield, both of whom had profited handsomely from acting in Wilde's plays, sealed their assistance of Queensberry's efforts by inviting several persons to a banquet to celebrate the marquess's success.

At a relatively quiet point in the festivities, Brookfield stood and was about to propose a toast to the honored guest. Just as he raised his glass there appeared at the entrance of the banquet room a woman of commanding presence. She was dressed in splendid Persian attire and accessories which, with her regal bearing, struck all the party as beautifully dramatic.

Queensberry saw her and immediately stood. "Madame Marisepehr, welcome to our party." Addressing the others around the table, he said: "Gentlemen, I wish to introduce to you a charming woman who deserves as much credit as anyone else in bringing Oscar Wilde to justice." The others at the table rose and began clapping. Queensberry then turned toward Marisepehr and raised his glass. "I propose a toast to this charming lady." He took a great swallow of his wine, and the others followed him in the toast.

Then Marisepehr stepped in front of Queensberry. "My lord, may I join you in this toasting ritual?"

"Of course," exclaimed Queensberry. "Will someone please bring Madame a glass? And make a place for her at the table."

"No, Lord Queensberry, I don't have time to stay. A glass of wine will be quite sufficient."

Someone handed Queensberry a wine glass which he filled with champagne and set before her. She took it, looked around at the group, and said: "I propose a toast to one of the most remarkable men I have ever known. He is kind, generous, amusing, and accomplished. I wish him well and can only regret that I seem at present powerless to help him." She then raised her glass and said, "To Mr. Oscar Wilde!" She took a small sip of the wine and let her gaze sweep the entire group of shocked, silent diners.

Fixing her eyes on Hawtrey and Brookfield, who were seated next to Queensberry, she said: "Actors, are you? Well, I hope your acting is generally better than it has been recently. Do you remember Hamlet's gentle praise of Yorick? *'A fellow of infinite jest, of most excellent fancy'*! So was Mr. Wilde, who I am sure would be able to do justice, verbally, to this disgusting situation! *Queensberry, Hawtrey, and Brookfield*! A most noble trio! My own command of English is totally inadequate to express my opinion of what you have done. But I remember a few lines from Shakespeare that come close:

'O villains, vipers, damn'd without redemption!
Dogs, easily won to fawn on any man!
Snakes, in my heart-blood warm'd, that sting my heart!
Three Judases, each one thrice worse than Judas!'"

Having said that, she looked at the entire group. "*All* of you ought to be ashamed of what you have done. To the extent that any of you are remembered in years to come, it will be because Oscar Wilde will be remembered, and *honoured*, far more." Then, stepping closer to Queensberry, she looked squarely at him: "And as for you, *My Lord Marquess*, let me tell *your* fortune. Whether you choose to believe me or not, I predict that you will not live to see the new century." With that she threw the rest of her wine into his stunned face, then set her glass on the table and left the room.

Queensberry's problems did not end with his encounter with Marisepehr. When, after the festivities, he, Hawtrey, and Brookfield exited the building in which the victory banquet had been held, he met his son Alfred as the latter staggered along in his distress and his intoxication. Father and son looked at each other with extreme hatred. Bosie spoke first.

"I suppose you're very proud of yourself!"

"Yes, indeed!" exclaimed the marquess, who was himself feeling the effects of his champagne. "I've never done a better day's work!"

"What a funny little man you are!" snarled Bosie.

"Why, you slimy scoundrel! I wonder who your *real* father is?"

"*So do I!*" shouted Bosie as he swung his umbrella at his father and knocked his hat off.

The infuriated marquess lunged at his son and, to the consternation of his two companions, managed to deliver several blows with his cane. Queensberry knocked his son down, but Bosie caught hold of his father's legs and pulled his feet from under him. There on the pavement they struggled drunkenly and traded blows and epithets until a policeman, having heard the fracas, quickly arrived, arrested them, and took them to the police station. In light of recent events and the lack of any serious injuries, the officers, trying to hide their amusement, released both men on their promise to keep the peace.

Though Alfred Douglas had promised that his family would pay Wilde's court costs, they did not. Queensberry's insistence that he be paid £600 for his court costs, as well as other creditors' demands, precipitated bankruptcy proceedings against Wilde's estate in late April. Constance Wilde and her two small sons were forced to flee to avoid not only this event but also the embarrassment that had fallen upon the family.

Those who witnessed it said that it was almost an orgy of activity at the Wilde home in Tite Street. Legal functionaries, bargain hunters, and curious members of the public paraded through the home. There were expensive pieces of furniture and fine *objets d'art*. First editions of books, many of them inscribed by the authors, were pawed over, gawked at, and sometimes damaged. Valuable letters and manuscripts were trampled upon. In no time at all the beautiful house was another victim of this barbarous, pathetic event.

Watson and Ross were appalled at the sight. They paused briefly across the street from number 16 and gazed in disbelief at the sight.

"Dr. Watson, would you mind very much if we tried to get inside?"

Watson glanced at Ross and shook his head. "No, I'm willing to go. Maybe we can manage to save something."

Both men moved slowly across the street and stepped inside the house. They gingerly picked their way past many others.

Ross pointed to one room. "That's Oscar's study." Followed by Watson, he made his difficult way over to the entrance.

Like most of the rest of the building, the study was chaotic. The bookshelves had been roughly treated, with some volumes lying on their sides and others on the floor. One, that had been kicked some distance away from its shelf, attracted Watson's attention. He picked it up and discovered that it was a first edition of the play *Callirrhoe*, by Michael Field.

"Mr. Ross, are you familiar with this author?"

Ross took the book, glanced at the title page, and leafed through the volume. "Oh, yes, that's by Oscar's good friends Katharine Bradley and Edith Cooper. They write under the pen name Michael Field." He pointed to the center of the title page where Wilde had written his name and the date, 1884.

Ross handed the book back to Watson, who took it over to someone apparently there in an official capacity. "Excuse me, my good man. How much is this?"

The man examined the volume quickly and handed it back. "Five shillings."

"Good, I'd like to buy it." Watson paid him the requested amount and was given a receipt.

Chapter 7

Sherlock Holmes and John Watson occasionally heard reports about Wilde's imprisonment. Some of them were mere rumours, but a few were from more trustworthy sources. There was little in any of them to raise the spirits of anyone who pitied Wilde and wished to make his difficult situation less onerous.

In the middle of 1896 Robert Ross and Bernard Shaw called upon Holmes and Watson. Reports about Wilde's prison tribulations had become more dire and pathetic, and the two men had been calling upon many of Wilde's friends, especially those socially or professionally prominent, to ask whether they would sign a petition to try to get more humane treatment for him.

"Holmes," said Shaw, "I recall that a few years ago I approached Wilde about signing a petition for the reprieve of the anarchists, who through questionable methods had been convicted of causing the Haymarket Riot in Chicago in 1886."

"And did he?" asked Holmes.

"He was almost the only distinguished person who did, and it earned my undying gratitude."

"My impression of him is that of a very kind and generous man," said Watson, "and I would be honoured to sign such a petition."

"As would I," said Holmes. "I regret very deeply that he let himself be pushed into taking the reckless action that he did. But he has become a victim of our revoltingly hypocritical society. That a man such as Wilde should spend two years in prison while the Marquess of Queensberry and his sort should be at large is a grotesque parody of justice. Wilde's behavior was foolish, but our society's has been far worse."

"Well, we have taken enough of your time," said Shaw. "The Reverend Mr. Stewart Headlam and I are going to call a meeting of those in London who would be willing to seek kinder treatment for Wilde. I need hardly say that we would be delighted if you both could attend. And feel free to bring anyone you think would offer support."

Ross observed that unless such a petition had an impressive number of respected names, it would be a futile gesture. He and Shaw then rose to leave, and Holmes and Watson stood also.

"We shall certainly attend!" exclaimed Watson. "I'm pleased to know that someone is trying to bring serious pressure to bear on the government in this matter."

"If our men of letters and other accomplished individuals won't respond," said Shaw, "I doubt that we can expect much from the nation as a whole. I'll certainly let you know when and where the meeting will be held. And I thank both of you gentlemen for letting us drop by and burden you with this commitment."

Ross expressed his appreciation, and Watson and Holmes assured their visitors that they were honored to be allowed to help in this matter. Shaw promised them that he would see that they had an opportunity to examine the draught of a petition as soon as it could be written.

A few weeks later Shaw was able to advise his list of friends and acquaintances when and where a meeting would be held for those interested in justice for Wilde. The invitation did not draw a large group, but it included several very respected persons in London and England. Not all of them supported such a petition, but most had opinions on the subject and all were at least curious about what might come of the effort.

Shaw asked Father Headlam to preside; but while he still had the floor, Shaw reminded the group that Wilde had been convicted under somewhat less than ideal legal conditions.

"That may well be," exclaimed Pre-Raphaelite painter Holman Hunt; "but Wilde was not—shall we say?—normal."

Shaw chuckled. "None of us is! There is no such thing as a *normal* human being. No, indeed! We all vary greatly from a mythical normality and display a great variety of *ab*normalities. Mr. Holmes over there can solve mysteries where I and most others don't even see mystery. And you, Mr. Hunt, can do things with paints that would be totally beyond even *my* greatest efforts. Fortunately, the term *normal human* is metaphysical fiction. If it weren't, I'd be in a devil of a situation when I try to write a play."

Hunt was unconvinced. "I still believe that the government has treated Wilde with great leniency."

Father Headlam leaned forward and looked keenly at Hunt. "You have become famous for your many paintings with religious themes. Have you no compassion for someone who has already suffered so grievously?"

"If I did what you wish," replied Hunt, "I would have to deny all individual responsibility for sinfulness. And, Father Headlam, are you, a priest in the Church of England, willing to condone what Wilde did?"

"In all my searching of the Gospels," said Headlam, "I have never found that Christ had anything to say on the subject. The nearest to this that I can recall is the account of the woman accused of adultery. Jesus handled that with little more than a tut-tut. Now, on this subject Paul and some other apostles presumed to hold forth at length—to put it mildly—which merely illustrates again how religious leaders have often had to pray for protection from their disciples."

"But," objected Hunt, "that's no proof that Our Lord approved of unnatural behavior."

"Nor that he disapproved," said Headlam. "One may, of course, suppose that he did; but supposition proves nothing." The priest then turned to Henry James, the American-born novelist and playwright. "Mr. James, what is your position on this matter?"

As James rose slowly from his seat, Frank Harris turned to More Adey and whispered, "Get ready for James to travel every byway in getting to his point."

"If I were forced," said James, "to make a categorical statement about this—if my back were against the wall, as it were—I would have to say—grasping the larger subject, you understand—I would have to say that I don't believe any such petition would have any effect on—that is, alter the attitudes of—the authorities in England. Dear me, no! They even object to—nay, *condemn*—the measurably less offensive works of such writers as Paul Bourget and Emile Zola."

"I suppose you refer to such a work as Zola's *Nana*," said Shaw.

Seeming to resent the actual mention of one of the offending works, James looked askance at Shaw and said, "Yes, that is one of M. Zola's more extravagant works. Its main character is drawn from the less admirable areas of Parisian life."

"She was a prostitute," said Shaw with a slight chuckle.

James again cast a pained glance at Shaw and paused as though trying to decide how best to respond to such directness. With a disdainful nod at Shaw, James said, "Yes, she was, as Mr. Shaw bluntly puts it, a *femme du pavé*." Obviously wishing to resume his seat, James ended tersely. "Therefore, gentlemen, Mr. Wilde's writings—some of them but not all, you understand—are so much worse than M. Zola's that such a petition would be simply a sort of manifesto by Wilde's closest friends." He started to sit but straightened up long enough to look around at the others and add, "And I was *never* one of them."

As James took his seat, Watson turned to Holmes and whispered, "James has never forgiven Wilde's success with *The Importance of Being Earnest*, at the St. James's Theatre, when his own *Guy Domville* had just failed at the same theatre." Holmes smiled and nodded.

Frank Harris, who had remained uncharacteristically quiet up to this point, broke into the discussion. "I was just recently telling Mr. Shaw that I've sounded out a few individuals who I thought might be willing to participate in this effort. But I had no luck at all. Jules Renard, for instance, told me that he had never cared for Wilde, but that he would sign such a petition if Wilde would give his word of honour never again to put pen to paper." This brought a few sounds of amusement from the group. "And George Meredith flatly refused to sign," he added.

After the meeting broke up, Shaw, Headlam, Harris, Holmes, Ross, and Watson met to discuss what to do in light of the paucity of those interested enough to sign a petition for Wilde's benefit.

"Well, gentlemen," observed Shaw, "it would appear that we are optimists of the most imaginative sort." With a sweeping gesture of his hand around their group, Shaw laughed and said: "We half-dozen! And one-third of these six are Headlam and I, perhaps the two most famous crackpots in the nation. That would at once tell British society that any effort for a petition for leniency is not to be taken seriously."

After Wilde was convicted, he was taken briefly to Pentonville Prison and then to Wandsworth Prison, where he spent six months of his two-year sentence. Then he went to Reading Gaol, the prison with which his name is most associated. In order to avoid any hecklers that Queensberry might have sent to Reading on his release date, Wilde was taken again, briefly, to Pentonville on 18 May 1897. There, early the next morning, he walked into freedom. More Adey and the Rev. Stewart Headlam had a brougham waiting for him.

The three greeted one another warmly, and Wilde stepped into the carriage that was closed to allow him privacy. After the three men had seated themselves, Wilde glanced over to an empty seat and saw a copy of the *Daily Chronicle*. He picked it up, looked at it, and laughed. "Do you know that one of the punishments the prison uses is to deprive one of the right to read the *Daily Chronicle*? Even yesterday, on the train from Reading to Pentonville, I asked whether I might read it. The warders said no. I asked whether I might at least read it upside down, and they consented." He chuckled and added, "Do you know, I never enjoyed it so much. It's the only way to read a newspaper."

Headlam and Adey laughed, but they were feeling very diffident, almost fearful that anything they might say would be inappropriate. Very soon, however, it was clear that Wilde was not at all sensitive on the subject of his last two years.

"Mr. Wilde," said Headlam, "I must say that you look quite well. You appear to have borne up well under what must have been terrible conditions."

"Oh, certainly sometimes it was difficult, even horrible. I shall write something on the subject." He smiled and gestured toward the newspaper beside him. "Perhaps the *Daily Chronicle* would publish it." Wilde pushed aside a curtain over the window nearest him and looked casually at the passing scenes. "My dear friends, I hope to learn to say, with absolute conviction, that the two great turning points in my life were when my father sent me to Oxford and society sent me to prison." He looked at his companions and noticed their surprise. "No, really, I'm quite serious. I learned a great deal in both places about both the world and myself, especially about myself. Obviously, Oxford was far more agreeable, both physically and intellectually. But perhaps the lesson from prison is more profound. Throughout my last two years I kept remembering something that Goethe wrote:

Who never ate his bread in sorrow,
Who never spent the midnight hours
Weeping and waiting for the morrow,
He knows you not, ye heavenly powers.

"How were the other prisoners?" asked Adey.

"Much more human, often, than the officials. The officers, the routine, and the physical facilities are designed to degrade one. Hard plank beds that produce insomnia, barely edible food that scarcely sustains one and brings diarrhoea. And there is a lack of decent reading materials and adequate medical attention. If this is how Her Majesty treats her prisoners, she doesn't deserve to have any!"

"But Reading Gaol," Wilde continued, "was an improvement over Wandsworth, especially after the arrival of Major Nelson as warden. And several of the warders were humane. Some even occasionally tried to engage me in literary matters. One in particular sounded me out about Dickens, as to whether he could be regarded as a great writer. I assured him he would, because he was no longer alive."

"'And John Strange Winter, sir; would you tell me what you think of him, sir?'"

"'A charming lady,' I said, 'he is a charming lady; but I would rather talk to *her* than read *his* books.'"

"'Thank you, sir. I did not know he was a lady, sir. Excuse me, sir, but Marie Corelli; would she be considered a great writer, sir?'"

"This," said Wilde, "was really more than I could bear. I put my hand on his shoulder, looked grave, and replied, 'Now, don't think I've anything against her *moral* character; but from the way she writes, she ought to be in *here*.'"

"'You say so, sir, you say so?' said the warder, apparently not doubting my assessment."

Adey and Headlam laughed at their friend's anecdotes. But Wilde felt very much in suspense and lacking in information about his immediate future.

"Now," said Wilde, "may I ask what I may expect once we get downtown?"

"Well," said Headlam, "we shall go to my home where some of your closest friends will welcome you back to London."

"I'm sure I shall be delighted to see them all," said Wilde. "I just wish that it did not have to be in London. I have no intention of remaining here. As soon as possible I shall be in France, where civilisation has not yet been proscribed. More, I think you, Robbie Ross, and Reggie Turner know my feelings on this matter."

"Yes, Oscar, and we have made some tentative plans. After you've met Mr. and Mrs. Leverson and a few others at Father Headlam's, we'll tell you what we've learned about possible places for you to live in France."

Wilde and his two friends reached Headlam's home and left the carriage. Headlam glanced about and was thankful that it was still too early for more than a few people to be up and about. He invited Adey and Wilde into his home. The recent prisoner glanced about and found the surroundings an almost overpowering scene. Filled with emotion, Wilde managed to say, "I had forgotten how beautiful such as this could be."

"Well, Mr. Wilde, I want you to feel completely at home."

"I shall certainly try, Father Headlam. I know now that I no longer have a home in London; my bankruptcy has seen to all that. And I believe my wife and sons are on the Continent. So, if you don't mind, I'm going to accept your kind offer and pretend that, at least for a few minutes, this is my home."

"Of course. And breakfast has been prepared for all of us. So, if you'll just step into the dining room, we'll let you have your first meal in freedom."

Wilde was overcome with emotion but managed to smile gratefully at the priest and then followed Headlam into the dining room. His host seated him at the head of the table and then sat immediately to Wilde's left. Adey took his place at Wilde's right.

Despite the two difficult years of imprisonment Wilde quickly became once again the delightful fellow of past times. He showed that he was not reluctant to discuss his recent experiences. "I shall certainly do some writing on the subject of prison reform," he exclaimed. "I'll go into particulars, too; but generally I could sum up the needed changes by saying that we need to civilise the prisons, humanise the wardens—and Christianise the chaplains."

"So, you had some contact with the clergy?" asked Headlam.

"Unfortunately, yes. Every so often a priest of the Established Church would drop by. He rarely had much to say, and even that little seemed to lack conviction."

Adey asked whether the priests ever inquired into Wilde's personal beliefs.

"Rarely. Oh, I recall that right after I was imprisoned a priest asked me whether there had been family prayers at my home. Upon my saying that there had not, he said sternly, 'You see where you are now!'" Wilde chuckled. "He then handed me a little tract and left. When I looked at it, I was struck by the irony that it dealt with the passage in Second Corinthians: '*Who also hath made us able ministers of the new testament; not of the letter, but of the spirit: for the letter killeth, but the spirit giveth life.*'"

"He probably wouldn't have liked Our Lord," said Headlam with a wry smile.

After they had finished breakfast, they sat talking in the parlour. Presently there was a knock at the door; and when Headlam answered it, the Leversons entered and quickly walked over to Wilde. He rose and greeted them warmly. To Ada he exclaimed: "Sphinx, how charming of you to know exactly the correct hat to wear early in the morning when greeting a friend who has been away!" Shaking his head in pleased admiration, he said, "I am filled with wonder and joy that you have risen so early to see me, even though sphinxes are minions of the moon."

Wilde told Headlam that he wanted to ask a nearby Jesuit monastery whether they would permit him to stay with them for a six-month retreat, which would give him a peaceful period in which to meditate and plan his future. Wilde wrote a letter to the monastery asking for such permission, and Headlam dispatched a courier with the letter. In a short while the messenger returned with a reply. Wilde read it, dropped his head, and handed it to Headlam, who read it aloud: "'Though we must refuse your request, we suggest that you ponder this matter for a year. Then, if you are still interested, we shall reconsider your request.'" Wilde broke down and wept bitterly but presently shook off the mood.

"Very well. I shall have to find my own solution to the problem of returning to society." With a faint smile he glanced about the group. "I'm sure that this is, after all, the best course for me to take."

Ada Leverson walked over to Wilde and put her arm around him. "Oscar, I don't think you will have any trouble with society. After all, you are the very spirit of society; you carry it with you. If you fail, then society is the loser, not you."

Dr. Watson returned home after visiting a patient. He saw several letters in the mailbox, picked them up, and mounted the stairs to his residence. As he relaxed in his chair, he thumbed through the several items and noticed that one came from Dieppe, France. He recognized Robbie Ross's handwriting and quickly opened the envelope. In his letter Ross explained that he would shortly return to London and that he wished to discuss with Holmes and Watson a matter of some importance. Watson immediately wrote a reply to assure Ross that they would be delighted to see him at any time after his arrival.

A few days later Ross found himself seated in the same chair he had occupied on his first visit to 221-B Baker Street. He eagerly told Holmes and Watson about Wilde's new home in the little village of Berneval-sur-Mer, a short distance northeast of Dieppe. Reginald Turner and Robbie had helped him get settled, at least for the present. Now back in London, Ross had a somewhat knotty problem and hoped that Watson and Holmes might be able to help him decide what course to take.

Robbie had brought with him a large, bulky envelope which at once caught his two friends' attention. When he opened it, he produced a stack of twenty folio sheets of blue-ruled paper, each sheet folded once. Ross's two friends could see at once that the sheets were filled with writing.

"Well, that's some very impressive-looking writing," said Watson. "Is it yours, Mr. Ross?"

"No, it's Oscar's, and I think it's one of the best things he's done." Ross went on to explain that it was a long letter to Bosie Douglas and that Wilde had written it while in Reading Prison. "When Oscar was released, this was returned to him. He asked me to take care of it and have two typed copies made of it. I was to keep one copy and to send the other to Douglas."

"And you did so?" asked Holmes.

"Yes."

Holmes asked whether Douglas knew that Ross had it. "Yes, I've given him his copy. My understanding is that he read only a few sentences and then in anger threw the entire thing into the fireplace. Apparently he believes that was the only copy."

"Does he know about the original document?" asked Watson.

"Apparently not, and I don't think I'm going to enlighten him. He'd merely try to gain possession of it and then tear it up; and I think it might very profitably be published."

"A private letter written to him?" asked Holmes.

"Well, what I'd do is go through the manuscript and remove everything that refers to him. Much of Oscar's letter is written without any explicit or implied references to Bosie." Ross picked up his typed copy and glanced at it. He tapped it with an index finger and said, "I can certainly understand why Bosie would be angry to read this." He laid the copy down, then leaned forward and clasped his hands. Looking from one man to the other, he explained what he saw as his difficult future project.

"Gentlemen, I'm very certain that much of this manuscript would make a good book, one that would find a market at once, especially if it bears Oscar's name. And for at least the immediate future Oscar is going to need to make as much money as he can. His estate is still complicated by his bankruptcy, and he has appointed me his literary executor. My job now is to try to pay off his legal debts and let him still have enough to live on. I hope to retrieve as many as possible of his literary properties."

"Have you thought of a title for this long letter," asked Watson.

"Yes, 'De Profundis,' for Oscar did indeed write it from the depths of prison and despair." Ross shook his head and said, "Oscar suggested another title, but I think it would be less satisfactory—a little clumsy. He wanted the title to be 'In Carcere et Vinculis.'"

Holmes looked at Ross and then Watson. "It has been years since I worked with Latin, but I think the first words mean *in prison*; I don't recognize the second."

Watson spoke up. "*In fetters*, I believe. Isn't that correct, Mr. Ross?"

"Yes. As I say, his suggestion is certainly appropriate, but I think the shorter title is preferable."

Both of his hosts agreed that Ross's title was better, especially for a book intended to appeal to the general reader.

"Besides," said Holmes with a self-deprecating smile, "we don't wish to embarrass those who haven't kept up on their Latin."

During Wilde's three remaining years he lived precariously, shifting his meager possessions from place to place in France, Italy, and (briefly) in Switzerland. Eventually he established his residence in Paris at the Hôtel d'Alsace, rue des Beaux Arts, where the proprietor, Jules Dupoirier, showed great kindness to, and patience with, "Monsieur Sebastian Melmoth," the assumed name that Wilde used during his years of exile. Of the several persons who saw him occasionally and befriended him in various ways, none was as faithful and indispensable as were Robert Ross and Reginald Turner, both of whom had to find time for Wilde in their busy schedules. As the exile's health began to deteriorate, this became increasingly difficult. By the fall of 1900, the last year of the old century, Wilde's condition necessitated an operation on his ear. It was performed in his room at the hotel, just before his forty-sixth birthday. Ross, who had been planning to travel to Paris a bit later, stepped up his schedule and reached there in time for his friend's birthday in October.

After Wilde became able to move about with help, Ross took him out one evening to a café. The young man was appalled that his friend, whose health was already very uncertain, drank absinthe, a liqueur that at that time was regarded as so harmful to the body that it was illegal in many places. Wilde noticed Ross's disparaging glance.

"Don't you like absinthe, Robbie?"

"No, I don't dare drink it." He bent forward and added softly, "And you shouldn't either." With special emphasis he said, "Oscar, you are killing yourself."

"And what have I to live for, Robbie?" Wilde lifted his glass and stared at it with a grim smile. "The French call it *la fée verte.*"

"The Green Fairy!" exclaimed Ross. "What a deceptive name for so insidious a beverage!"

"Ah, but a very appropriate one for a drink of such magical properties." Wilde took a slow sip, then put the glass down. "Did you know, after one absinthe one sees the world as it isn't? After two one sees it as one wishes it were. And after three one sees it as it really is, and that is the worst of all."

"And you enjoy that?" asked Ross with a tone of incredulity.

"I enjoy the drama it offers."

"But, Oscar, why don't you go to a theatre to enjoy drama?"

"I can't afford the price of admission, Robbie. Besides, I can attend Mass and see drama, make-believe, and pageantry as good as the best theatres offer." He took another sip of his drink. "But my dear fellow, I've seen many Masses and all the best plays many times. I know them by heart and know exactly what to expect from them. But absinthe is entirely different; it is subtle and completely unpredictable. At any moment now I shall be able to glance at that woman over there and see her as something quite different from what she now seems to be. In fact, I already begin to see her as more like a street lamp wearing a shako. And after that—who knows? Perhaps she will soon become like a *danseuse* in a painting of the ballet by Monsieur Degas." With an almost pained facial expression he added, "Or perhaps after I've had my third absinthe, she will look like an Old Bailey judge passing sentence and enjoying every syllable of his terrible words."

Ross felt a pang of recollection as he glanced at his friend, and he quickly tried to change the mood. "Do you drink absinthe at your hotel, Oscar?"

"No, only on special occasions, and as a guest of kind friends, can I afford anything that expensive. But on my birthday recently someone brought me a bottle of champagne. I told him that he was forcing me to die beyond my means."

Wilde's face became serious. "Robbie, I think I don't have much time left. As much as I hate to burden you further, I should be very grateful if you would make all my funeral and burial arrangements."

Ross started to reply but, from a surge of emotion, had to stop.

Wilde reached out and patted his arm. "Now, don't let this kind of conversation assume more importance for you than it deserves. These are practical matters that we need to discuss. I've accomplished enough to satisfy myself that I've perhaps made some contribution to our national letters, if not today then perhaps in years to come. Besides, I doubt that I have anything more of importance to say. When I did my writing, I did not know life. I regarded it as simply a great comedy being performed, and I felt the need to reveal that to everyone—or *tout le monde*, as the French more aptly say it. But now I see that life for any individual ultimately becomes essentially a matter of a few special individuals. Mine has now been reduced to a handful, of whom you are certainly one." He smiled broadly and said with a flourish, "Robbie Ross, Friend of Friends."

"Oscar—" Ross had started to say something but stopped. In embarrassment he rubbed tears from his eyes.

Wilde leaned forward and said softly, "Now, Robbie, just think: If I die before the end of this year, it will be my first patriotic gesture to England." He chuckled . "After all, if I lived into the new century, it would really be more than the British public could bear." With a puckish smile he added, "But I may wait until the very last day of December."

Wilde paused and took a sip of absinthe, then leaned back in his chair. "And, Robbie, I also must remember an important fact, perhaps the *most* important fact for me at this late date."

"And what's that, Oscar?"

"Merely this: Death is one's final opportunity to perform an important task well. With your help, I don't see how I can fail to do that." He took another sip of his drink, slapped his hand lightly on the table, and exclaimed, "But, now to important details—and you must force yourself to discuss these with me without undue emotion. I've been talking with several

Parisians as to whether I might be buried in this city's Père Lachaise Cemetery."

Ross sat up and stared.

"You seem shocked." observed Wilde.

"No, just surprised. I think it would be an excellent place to be buried. It's only that the idea hadn't occurred to me."

"Well, I have been thinking about it, for then I would be a permanent resident in the world's most civilized city." His face assumed a very serious expression. "I've even been giving some thought to a proper memorial tomb."

"Really, Oscar? What sort of memorial would you like?"

"I see my monument as a great equestrian statue." Ross looked puzzled until Wilde added solemnly, "Yes, a great *rampant* equestrian statue."

The two men laughed heartily, and Ross gasped out, "With sword in hand!"

"Yes, that would almost make me a fifth horseman of the Apocalypse, wouldn't it?" Wilde laughed and added, "War, Fire, Pestilence, and Death. Now, what remains for me to represent?"

"Why couldn't you be the horseman who gives the lie to the other four?"

"Robbie, you must not be so clever!" said Wilde with approving laughter.

"But, Oscar, you're going to live much longer!"

"No, Robbie, my life has already become a melodrama. There have been plot, development, crisis, sensation, tragedy— everything in fact except a happy ending. Well, of course it will be happy for the British. At any rate, I fear anything more would be repetition, bathos, and anticlimax." He said this sombrely but then smiled and added: "However, I suppose the music halls need their entertainment, too. But, Robbie, if I'm going to be buried in Père Lachaise, the question arises as to where I'd like to be buried—who my neighbors would be."

"How about Héloïse and Abélard?"

"Indeed!" exclaimed Wilde, "that would be strangely appropriate, for both Abélard and I hazarded everything on love, and both of us lost. He was physically castrated, and I have been emasculated as an artist. We are both eunuchs."

Wilde was suddenly quiet and seemed deep in thought.

"Oscar, what are you thinking?"

Wilde sat up and took a generous sip of his drink, set it down, and smiled mischievously. "Robbie, when the last trumpet sounds, and we are couched in our porphyry tombs, I shall turn to you and whisper, 'Robbie, Robbie, let's pretend we don't hear it.'"

"Now, Oscar, you know I'm not a convincing liar."

Wilde smiled benignly. "That's because you're an honest man."

In London Sherlock Holmes returned home just as John Watson had finished reading a letter. After sitting down, Holmes glanced over at Watson. "A letter from Ross?"

Watson nodded. "Yes, he says that Wilde is probably not going to survive the year, perhaps not even this month." He put the letter back into its envelope and held it out to Holmes, who took it and scanned it quickly.

"Well, Watson, I know you have been considering paying Wilde a visit; so if you still intend doing that, I think you ought not to wait longer. I'd go with you except that I don't see how I could leave right at this time. I most assuredly offer my financial assistance. In fact, I'll pay your expenses if you would go there and represent both of us. Perhaps you might even be of some medical assistance."

Watson nodded. "I'm most appreciative, Holmes. Yes, I really do think I must go. From what I read in Ross's letters, I gather that Wilde is, and has been, in very desperate straits, both physically and financially. Almost the only ones who have been able to spend much time with him are Ross and Turner." To Holmes' question as to whether he would stay at Wilde's hotel, Watson said, "No, I'll go to my usual address. It's not far from the Hôtel d'Alsace."

After both men had sat for several moments in silence, Holmes said: "I'm very relieved that you wish to do this. This poor man's situation has bedevilled me greatly for the past five years."

Watson had notified Ross as to when he expected to reach Paris and where he would stay, and upon his arrival he immediately went to Wilde's hotel. Arriving shortly after noon, he was fortunate in finding the proprietor, M. Dupoirier, in his office. He immediately offered to escort Watson up to Wilde's room, where both Ross and Turner were sitting and talking with the patient. Clad in a robe Wilde lay on his bed with his head on a pillow propped against the headboard . After all the mutual greetings, Watson glanced around the room at the simple scene that was untroubled by any pretense to elegance. He made an encompassing gesture with his hand. "I say, Mr. Wilde, you seem to be very comfortably settled in here."

"And so must you be also, my dear fellow! Reggie, would you or Robbie bring that chair from my desk and set it over here for Dr. Watson?" Ross quickly did so and set it near Wilde's bed. Watson thanked him and sat.

"Well, Dr. Watson, in response to your statement that my quarters are comfortable, I can certainly assure you that though they are modest, they are quite an improvement over prison. My main complaint is the wallpaper."

Watson glanced at it and said with a smile, "I don't really have much aesthetic sense. However, yes, I do think I might have selected some other pattern."

"Indeed! As I commented the other day to my physician, the wallpaper and I are fighting a duel to the death. One of us has to go." Wilde then thanked Watson for taking the time and trouble to visit.

"I'd been planning for some time to do this. And by the way, Holmes very particularly wishes to be forgiven for his inability to be here just at present. He asked that I represent him, and he promises to be here himself as soon as possible."

Wilde smiled and nodded. "Dr. Watson, will you grant me a very great favor?"

"Of course."

"Then, may we dispense with last names. I'd regard it as an honour to enjoy a first-name acquaintance with you."

"I'd like that very much," said Watson, "even though I'm accustomed to calling male acquaintances by their last names. However, I like your suggestion. So, I'm John, and you are Oscar."

"Excellent!" said Wilde, "that's quite settled." With a chuckle he added, "Or would you prefer *Jack*, that 'notorious domesticity for John'?"

Everyone laughed at the allusion to Wilde's last play.

"I haven't been called John or Jack since public school!" said Watson. He then added quickly, "Well, both my wives did call me John." He turned toward Robbie and Reggie and said, "But this matter of first names is not quite settled. "May we include your two faithful friends in this arrangement? I'd like that too."

"So would I," exclaimed Turner. "And call me Reginald—or Reggie. Whichever you prefer."

"Then Reggie, it is," said Watson.

Wilde pointed to Ross. "And as for that young man, Robbie is the only possible first name. Ever since he was a schoolboy and lived with Constance and me in Tite Street, he has borne that diminutive, and thus has gone down in history. After all, what can one make of *Robert Baldwin Ross*? Who could that possibly be? It sounds dangerously like a prime minister or possibly even an archbishop of Canterbury. Ah, but *Robbie Ross*! Now, *that* is distinctive!"

In the middle of November Ross explained to Wilde that he was obliged to go to the south of France where his mother awaited him. Though Wilde begged him not to go, Ross was adamant; and Wilde gloomily predicted that he would never see Ross again. Fortunately, Reggie Turner was willing to carry on alone in attending the sick man. Watson could not have chosen a better time to arrive. It was also fortunate that Dr. Watson agreed to remain longer and to assist both as a friend and as a physician. But as the end of the month approached, Turner, who could see that Wilde was slipping away, notified Ross to return.

During these trying days another person, Fariedeh Marisepehr, learned of the stricken writer's condition. She left London at once and arrived in Paris on November twenty-fifth. She had not seen Wilde since before his trials, and she was appalled by his condition and appearance. Upon her arrival at the Hôtel d'Alsace, she introduced herself to the proprietor who checked the patient's room to see whether a female visitor might call. Wilde was in some pain but was delighted when his spiritualist advisor walked in.

"My dear Sybil," said Wilde with as much strength as he could muster, "you are indeed clairvoyant to know that I have been wishing to see you."

Neither Watson nor Turner recognised the visitor, and Wilde made the necessary introductions. He explained how much he had relied on her and what great help she had been during the trying days before his trials and imprisonment.

"And, gentlemen, I wish you to know that my beloved Sybil made a very spectacular appearance before Queensberry's victory banquet. I believe, dearest Madame Marisepehr, that you left them with a new appreciation of eloquence, irony, and dramatics in general. I wish only that it had not been necessary to waste that champagne on Queensberry. But, if it had to be so wasted, I wish it might have been an especially cheap *vin ordinaire.*"

Hardly had Wilde finished speaking when it was obvious that he was feeling great pain. Watson examined the patient and found him very feverish. He recommended that the two physicians who were already familiar with the case be summoned. After they had arrived and examined Wilde, they warned of the problem that could arise if the inflammation should go to his brain. Watson concurred in this view and in the inadvisability of another operation.

Soon the patient began to display moments of incoherence. He spoke in disconnected phrases, ramblings in French, or statements that indicated he was imagining himself back in his earlier life.

On one occasion when his presence of mind returned briefly, he gloomily said, "My friends, I have dreamt that I was feasting with the dead." Those standing around him were uncomfortable until Reggie Turner had the presence of mind to say, "My dear Oscar, I'm sure you were the life and soul of the party." Even Wilde had to laugh at this wonderful sally.

Spurred by Turner's pessimistic messages, Robbie Ross returned on the twenty-ninth to find Wilde unable to speak and clearly dying. The young man was uncertain about Wilde's desire to see a priest. It was obviously too late to expect the dying man to receive the Host or to make a confession. Besides, the latter's views on religion were certainly less than orthodox and Ross knew it. He suspected, however, that Wilde might receive some comfort from the presence of a Catholic priest. Moreover, reception into the Catholic Church would also make it easier for him to have a dignified funeral and burial. Perhaps Ross thought it providential that Wilde could not speak.

"Oscar, can you hear me?" asked Ross. Wilde opened his eyes slowly and raised his hand, a gesture which Ross interpreted as an affirmative reply. "Would you like me to bring a priest?" Wilde again raised his hand. Ross left and went quickly to the Passionist Fathers where he secured the services of Father Cuthbert Dunne, who spoke English. When Dunne asked Wilde whether he wished to be received into the Catholic Church, Wilde again raised his hand. Dunne then gave conditional baptism, absolution, and anointment. Early the next morning, the thirtieth, Ross, Watson, and Turner were startled to hear sounds suggesting that Wilde was dying. Almost immediately an examination revealed that he had. The men then proceeded to prepare Wilde's body properly, to clothe him in white linen, and to put a Rosary into his hands. Ross asked Maurice Gilbert, a friend of Wilde's, to take a flash photograph.

Fariedeh Marisepehr moved slowly over to the foot of Wilde's bed. While the others watched quietly and in fascination, she reached down and placed her hands on his lifeless feet. After a few seconds of apparent meditation she spoke.

"Oscar Wilde, you can be sure that you die a great man, though it may take much of the world a while to realise that. You have enriched your native language and letters with beauty, wit, and imagination. You have suffered at the hands of your society's basest and most illiberal elements, many of whom are guilty of an uncharitable and hypocritical outlook that is much worse than anything of which you have been accused. You have borne your troubles with dignity and even with the humour for which you are famed. It has been an honour to know you as a friend, and I bid you farewell. May you have peace at last."

She turned and walked away from the deathbed. Turner looked at Ross and whispered, "Now, *that* was the *genuine* absolution."

The End

Epilogue

My interest in Sherlock Holmes and Oscar Wilde goes back many years. When I was eleven years old, someone gave me a copy of *The Return of Sherlock Holmes*; and though I enjoyed the stories, I remember being puzzled about what a *pince-nez* was and how to pronounce the term. About nine years later I read Hesketh Pearson's excellent biography of Wilde and over the following years read all of Wilde's writings and the remaining Sherlock Holmes stories. In more recent years I have enjoyed the late Jeremy Brett's rendering of Sir Arthur Conan Doyle's famous detective. I still regard Brett's portrayal as the best.

In early 1955, while in the United States Air Force, I acquired a brief autographed note that Wilde wrote in June of 1882 while lecturing in Mobile, Alabama. With it came an original photograph of Wilde that, as I learned later, was one of many that New York photographer Napoleon Sarony took of the celebrated young visitor to America.* Later, it occurred to me that I could not recall seeing the photograph in any book about Wilde. I found the address of Wilde's surviving son, Vyvyan B. Holland, and sent him a copy of the picture with a letter asking whether he had seen it. He quickly replied that he had not and that he wished to use it in a biography he was writing of his father.** Not more than two days after mailing my letter, I was embarrassed to find the photograph in Frances Winwar's *Oscar Wilde and the Yellow Nineties*, a book I had read sometime earlier. At once I wrote again to Mr. Holland and apologized for the lapse of memory. He replied that the picture was nevertheless unfamiliar to him and that he still wished to use it.

At the start of our correspondence, Holland mentioned that he was helping Rupert (later *Sir* Rupert) Hart-Davis, London author and publisher, bring out a comprehensive collection of Oscar Wilde's letters. Wishing to have even a minor part in the project, I soon purchased four original letters, copies of which I sent to Holland. He thanked me and passed them on to Hart-Davis, who sent me his own thanks. In 1960 I decided to spend some months in Vienna, Austria, and both Holland and Hart-Davis invited me to call on them if I visited England. I did so after leaving Vienna. At noon on 9 May 1961 I called upon Mr. Holland, at his home in Sloane Street, and visited with him for about an hour. Two days later I spent much of the afternoon

---

* Both the autographed note and the photograph are in the Draughon Library, Auburn University, Auburn, Alabama. Wilde's note says: "Written in order to escape seeing reproach in beautiful Southern eyes at my lecture."

** Vyvyan B. Holland, *Oscar Wilde: A Pictorial Biography* (New York: Viking, 1960).

talking with Mr. and Mrs. Hart-Davis in their office. On 15 May I left Southampton, England, aboard the S. S. *America*.

While I haven't come to believe, as I understand some have, that Sherlock Holmes was an actual person, there is a little nook in my imagination where I enjoy seeing him as real. As for Wilde, he would be on my short list if allowed to summon some figure from the past. For that matter, so would Sherlock Holmes if I knew how to work it.

Fred W. Edmiston

10831096R0